THE LYME REGIS MURDER

Rachel McLean writes thrillers that make your pulse race and your brain tick. Originally a self-publishing sensation, she has sold millions of copies digitally, with massive success in the UK, and a growing reach internationally. She is the author of the Dorset Crime novels and the spin-off McBride & Tanner series and Cumbria Crime series. In 2021, she won the Kindle Storyteller Award with *The Corfe Castle Murders* and her books regularly hit No 1 in the Bookstat ebook chart on launch.

ALSO BY RACHEL MCLEAN

Dorset Crime series

RACHEL McLEAN

A DORSET CRIME SERIES NOVELLA

THE LYME REGIS MURDER

ACKROYD PUBLISHING

Ackroyd Publishing

ackroydpublishing.com

Printed and bound by CPI Group (UK) Ltd, Croydon, CR0 4YY

DORSET MURDER MAP

From the Dorset Crime series by Rachel McLean

N

Lyme Regis

Winfrith Police HQ

Wareham
Lesley's cottage

Blue Pool

Tyneham

Portland Bill

Bournemouth
Elsa's flat

Sandbanks

Brownsea Island

Old Harry Rocks

Corfe Castle

The Obelisk

The Globe

Illustration by Maria Burns

rachelmclean.com

CHAPTER ONE

JIM WOLLASON SHIVERED as he climbed out of his van, parked next to the lifeguard building at the entrance to Lyme Regis's famous Cobb. It was six am, only days until Christmas, and it was bloody freezing.

Pulling the van's back door open, he grabbed his coat; the warm one his daughter had given him last Christmas. He'd had the same old waterproof for years and had protested when she told him it wasn't enough, but he was damn glad of this one.

He zipped the coat up and made his way onto the Cobb. As he passed the door to the lifeguard station, it opened.

"Alright, Jim." It was Eddie, the station manager.

"Morning, Eddie. How's business?"

Eddie wrinkled his nose. "Quiet, so far. I don't like the look of that storm brewing out to sea, though."

"Brewing?" Surely the storm was already here.

Eddie chuckled. "This isn't a storm, mate. This is the kind of weather where I can make myself a cuppa safe in the knowledge I'll get to finish it. You wait."

Jim shrugged. "OK. Let us know if it's too dangerous to operate the machinery, yeah?"

"You'll know that on your own."

Jim gave Eddie a nod and headed along the Cobb, taking the lower route. Only tourists and idiots – often the same thing – took the top route, especially in winter. The stones up there slanted precariously to one side and were often slippery. Perfect conditions for falling off, and half of what kept Eddie and his lads busy.

Jim's supervisor, Geeta, was already there, crouched by the equipment, switching on the lights that made it possible for them to work this early. He knew some of the locals didn't appreciate bright lighting along the Cobb, but he also knew those same locals grumbled if they carried on working past mid-afternoon. So they started early, when the place was quiet. They were dredging the harbour, levelling its base so that the currents would behave more predictably once the spring tides came.

It was boring work, but it was paying for the holiday he had planned to Majorca with Brenda in May. He'd perused the brochure for the hundredth time before coming out; it was what kept him going on cold, dark mornings like this.

"Right," said Geeta. "We're moving to the area immediately by the harbour wall today. Hopefully the shelter means we won't have to knock off at lunchtime."

He grunted and climbed inside the cab of his machine. Legs protruded from each side, and it stood a little way back from the edge. Both he and Geeta knew how dangerous these things could be, and he was pleased to see she'd done all the safety checks before he'd arrived.

She was alright, Geeta. Didn't throw her weight around, like some supervisors he'd had. He'd been wary of working for a woman on a site like this, and a... well, an outsider, too. But she was better than most of the blokes he'd worked with.

He ran through the safety checklist, casting his eyes over buttons and lights, before cranking the machine's arm over the water. This was the risky bit; he'd known guys who hadn't set up properly, or who'd sited their gear on a slope, and ended up in the water. It was why he wasn't required to wear a seatbelt. If this thing toppled, he needed to be able to get out, and fast.

Slowly, glad to see that Geeta was watching from a safe distance, he let the arm swing out over the harbour. The tide was going out and the water level receding. That would make things easier for them. Dredging at high tide was a mucky business.

The digger hit the silt at the bottom of the harbour and began to move, picking up muck and debris as it went. His job was to shift it, pull it up, and dump it into the vast skip situated on the harbour wall.

He pulled at the lever and the machine's arm came up, dripping, seaweed hanging from it as always.

"Stop!"

He stopped the arm's movement, gently; he wasn't about to panic. He was wearing a hard hat and woolly beanie beneath, and Geeta's voice was muffled, but the urgency in it was unmistakable.

He waited. He knew better than to shift his weight or make the rig move any more than it needed to.

"What's up?"

She rounded the front of the machine so he could see her. "You've pulled something up."

He resisted a laugh. "Of course I've bloody pulled something up. That's my job."

She shook her head. Her face was pale. "Not silt, Jim. Something else."

He frowned. *What the hell?* "What?"

She pulled off her hard hat and scratched her head. She looked past him, towards the arm of the dredger. "I'm not... look." She frowned. "Bring it over onto the harbour wall. Drop it onto the ground."

"Not in the skip?"

She shook her head. "It wouldn't be... I'm not sure..." She put her hard hat back on, her movements jerky. "Just put it on the ground, yeah? Then secure the rig and get down. I need a second pair of eyes on this."

He shrugged and did as he was told. Geeta was being weird, but he trusted her. He secured the machine and climbed down from it.

She was standing next to the pile of debris he'd brought up.

"I was right," she said, pointing.

He followed her fingertip. "No."

"Yes," she said.

He took a step forward. Sticking out from the pile of silt and seaweed was something that looked very much like a leg.

"Shit," he said. "Has anyone gone off here recently?" He looked back towards the coast guard. "Is he... she... could they be alive?"

Geeta shook her head. "I saw more of it when you were bringing it in, Jim." She swallowed. Her face had gone a weird colour, and he knew it wasn't just because of the artificial lighting.

She looked at him.

"You've just pulled up a dead body, mate."

CHAPTER TWO

THERE WASN'T much that scared DC Tina Abbott. She'd calmed down drunks intent on giving her a slap, seen more than her fair share of dead bodies, and once she'd even pulled a very irate swan out of the River Frome.

But all those things paled into insignificance beside the prospect of Annie Abbott in a bad mood.

They were walking down Lyme Regis's Broad Street towards the sea and the gargantuan Christmas tree, Tina holding her son Louis's hand and her mum, Annie, striding ahead. The shops were decked out with the usual Christmas trees above the doorways, and the smell of mulled wine and roasting chestnuts filled the air. It was the second week in December and the town was full of visitors.

Tina had wanted to tell her mum that she and her husband Mike were planning to spend Christmas with Mike's mum in Poole, and that it might be the last chance for them to do so. She'd wanted to wait until she and Annie were settled in the Cobb Arms later that evening, but her mum had insisted on coming into town to do the shopping, and the conversation had turned to how many she'd be catering for on the big day.

"Louis, do you want to look in the toy shop?" Annie asked, not turning round. They were standing outside the Old Forge, which was a fossil shop, not a toy shop. But Tina wasn't about to contradict her.

Tina squeezed her son's hand. "In a minute, love."

Annie had been in a hurry, and they'd left the house without Tina even having a chance to put her bag down, let alone change out of her work clothes. She was still wearing a white shirt and plain trousers, and she felt drab and out of place among the explosion of Christmas cheer. Annie, of course, was wearing a garish Christmas jumper: one of her collection of ten which came out of storage on November 1st every year.

Annie eyed Tina. "So, what does Mike want for Christmas?"

Tina bit her lip. She'd been trying to get Mike to tell her all week, but he'd just shrugged and told her not to worry, that he'd be happy with whatever she chose. In the end, she'd gone for a scarf from one of the outdoor shops. A safe bet.

She took a deep breath. "I'm getting him a scarf," she said.

Annie frowned. "That's it?"

"It's a nice one," Tina said. "Wool, soft. He'll like it."

Annie sniffed. "You could have got him a scarf from anywhere. I wanted to get you all something special."

Tina felt her shoulders tense. "That's all he asked for."

Annie put a hand on Tina's arm. "I know, love. I'm just worried about you." She looked down. "I... I'll miss you." Her gaze flicked up. "But I do understand. With Carmen being..."

Tina nodded. Annie didn't like talking about illness. She

believed herself invincible and was probably judging Mike's poor mum for not being the same.

"Don't worry, Mum," she said. "It's going to be fine. We're going to have a lovely time."

They'd spend next Christmas with Annie, Tina had promised her. But this was the first Christmas in her life she hadn't been here in Lyme Regis, and she knew it rankled. Tina sighed, then turned at a flash that had caught her eye.

"What's that?"

"Don't change the subject."

Louis pulled at Tina's arm. "Fossil!"

She smiled down at him. "Yes, love. Ammonite."

"Ammite."

She laughed. But the blue flash she'd spotted at the top of Broad Street was nearing. "That's a police car," she said.

Annie put a hand on her arm. "You're off duty, love. And it's probably just Christmas lights."

Tina felt her jaw clench. *I know police lights when I see them.*

Sure enough, a police car emerged from Silver Street and glided down the road towards Cobb Gate car park, vehicles swiftly moving out of its way.

"I need to go and see," Tina said. "I might be able to help."

"You're off duty!"

Off duty. Lyme Regis never saw blue lights. It wasn't that kind of place. *Hang off duty.*

"Mum," she said. "Please. Just take Louis for a minute." Her brother-in-law Dougie *was* on duty. He might be in that car, and Annie knew it.

Annie huffed but grabbed her grandson's hand. "Let's go get a hot chocolate, Lou-lou."

He grinned.

Tina turned to see the police car making its way back up the road. Its lights were flashing but the sirens were silent.

"See?" said Annie. "No sirens. Not an emergency."

No, but...

Tina looked at her mum. "Please."

Annie shook her head. "Alright, then. But make sure you're home for tea."

She grinned at her mum. "Thanks."

"Yeah, yeah."

Tina ran up the hill, after the car, pulling her phone from her pocket as she went.

CHAPTER THREE

DCI Lesley Clarke stood in Superintendent Carpenter's pale-walled office in the new Dorset Police HQ building at Winfrith. She knew what he was about to tell her: she wasn't spending enough time behind a desk.

He'd been happy enough for her to get her hands dirty when she'd only been leading the Major Crimes Investigation Team. But following her success in the DCI Mackie investigation – a success that remained officially unacknowledged – he'd decided she needed more responsibility. So she now had two teams: the MCIT, and the new Cold Cases Team.

Which meant she was expected to take a step back and manage.

She shuddered.

She leaned forward, placing a hand on the desk, then withdrew it at a look from Carpenter. "But one of those teams doesn't have a DI yet, sir."

He raised a hand as his phone rang. "That's a temporary issue."

He was right. A DI had been recruited to head the MCIT: Hannah Patterson. Lesley wasn't much looking forward to working with her.

He looked at her. "You've got two teams now, Lesley. You can manage them from right here."

She shifted from foot to foot. She'd been up since six and could feel her stomach rumbling. She wished she'd grabbed something from the vending machine on her way in.

"Sir..." she began.

He held up a hand and answered his ringing phone. She stood there, clenching and unclenching a fist in her pocket.

He put down the phone and looked at her.

She held her breath, waiting. What was that all about? A way to assert his authority? To keep her waiting?

Carpenter had been weird with her in the fifteen months since she and her team had solved the Fran Dugdale case, and finally established how her predecessor DCI Tim Mackie had died. Power plays, mood swings, asking her to do things that really weren't her job.

What now?

He raised an eyebrow. "I've got a case for you. A body's been found in Lyme Regis harbour. Pretty bad state, by the sound of things. Could be one for your Cold Cases Team."

She nodded. "Jill's first case." DI Scott had been recruited over a year ago, but funding issues and the building of the new HQ across from the old mid-century building they'd occupied until just under six months ago had meant delays. Jill had only actually started a week ago.

Carpenter sniffed. "She's SIO, not you. You need to stay in the office and coordinate activity."

Lesley tightened her grip around a piece of fluff she'd found in her pocket. At least, she hoped it was fluff.

"Yes, sir."

He gave her a wave: *dismissed.* She turned for the door, her shoulders slumping.

If she wasn't investigating cases, then what was the point?

CHAPTER FOUR

ANNIE STOOD on the harbour wall, looking past the lifeboat station towards the Cobb. There were boats out there, boats she didn't normally see on her walks down here. And immediately in front of her was a line of police tape.

Tina was up there somewhere, having not reappeared since she'd left Annie in Broad Street. Louis was in his pushchair, sleeping. Good job, too: this wasn't a place for a little 'un like him.

She squinted to see if she could get a better view, but it was no use.

"Bugger. Should have brought my binoculars." She sighed and turned towards the town, realising a small crowd had gathered behind her. She nodded at a few she knew: Jay, who worked at the fossil shop they'd been standing outside earlier, and her neighbour Howard.

"You know what's going on, Annie?" Jay asked.

She shook her head. "My Tina's over there somewhere, but I've no idea what it's about."

"They've found someone in the water," said a woman she didn't recognise.

Annie frowned at her. "Really?"

The woman shrugged. "Just what I heard."

Annie knew how these things worked; rumours spread through a crowd like this faster than butter on a slice of toast. She'd wait until she could speak to Tina. She owed the girl an apology, anyway.

And Louis would be wanting his tea soon.

She scanned the crowd. Was it worth going home and getting her binoculars? Or would that make her a nosy parker?

There were no police at the cordon. She eyed it. It would be so easy just to lift the thing and walk through. As she put out a hand, a man appeared from the lifeboat station.

He gave her a suspicious smile. "Annie Abbott, how did I know you'd be causing trouble?"

"Me? Never." She returned the smile. She'd known Tim forever; they'd attended the same school and both lived here in Lyme all their lives. What Tina didn't know was that her mother had dated him before meeting the girls' dad. If it hadn't been for Brian, maybe she and Tim...

"I know when I'm not wanted," she told him, stepping back and lowering her hand. "But can you tell me what's going on?"

She felt the crowd behind her, pressing forward. He glanced over her head. "Sorry, Annie. Everyone. Now if you don't mind all moving along, the vehicles need access. You know how it is."

She did. They all did. You didn't live in a seaside town and not respect the needs of the lifeboat chaps.

"Right, Tim. When Tina comes past, tell her I've taken the little 'un home, will you?"

"Course, Annie." He tipped his cap. She liked Tim. Old-fashioned. She'd been widowed now for four years, and she wasn't completely over the hill yet.

She watched Tim walk away from her towards the Cobb. She squinted: was Tina that figure moving around over there? Her daughter had been wearing dark colours over the white shirt, and from here, it was impossible to tell.

She considered phoning her for a moment – she had dumped Louis on her, after all – then thought better of it.

"Come on, big fella," she said to the sleeping child. "Let's go home."

She navigated the pushchair through the crowd and made her way up Cobb Road. She'd take a route through town, along Hill Street and past the police station. See if Dougie was there.

She was just getting onto the steep bit when she saw a woman round the corner ahead of her.

The woman raised a hand. "Annie, that you?"

"Of course it's me." Annie stopped pushing, waiting for her friend to make her way down the hill. Going home could wait. "Have you seen what's going on at the Cobb?"

Rosamund shook her head. "No. What?"

Annie grinned. "Follow me."

She'd seen Rosamund around town for years, but only befriended her after they'd both joined the small group of women who swam in the bay every morning. Annie, Rosamund, Figgy and Helen. Rosamund was wealthy, or at least she seemed to be. She lived in a big house on the edge of town with a husband Annie had still never met.

"There are police boats out there," she said. "Word is, they've found a body."

Rosamund trotted along behind her, struggling to keep up with Annie, who had the momentum of the pushchair on her side. "Is your son-in-law involved?"

"Dougie? No idea. But Tina's there." Annie pushed through the crowd again and stopped to point out the boats clustered around the Cobb at the point where it curved round to the left.

"Tina?" Rosamund said, her eyes on the scene in front of them. "She's visiting?"

Annie beamed. Rosamund had a son, but he was nothing like her Tina. "She is. I've got little Lou-lou this afternoon, too." She didn't mention that she hadn't exactly volunteered to babysit.

Rosamund pulled in a breath. "They're pulling something out of the water."

"Are they?" Annie screwed up her eyes. Did she need specs?

She had a thought. *Annie Abbott, you're a genius.*

She pulled her phone out of her bag and raised it to her face, opening the camera app. She zoomed in.

That was...

"Oh my God."

"What?" Rosamund grabbed the phone. Annie grasped at it, but her friend was too tall.

"They are," Rosamund said. She lifted the cordon and took a few steps past the lifeboat station. "There's a body. Looks like they pulled it out of the harbour."

Stop, Annie wanted to tell her. But Tim was nowhere to be seen. Might as well join her.

She followed Rosamund under the cordon, briefly

tangling it in the pushchair before she stepped forward to stand by her friend. They were past the boatyard now, Monmouth Beach dropping down to her right.

She swallowed, hoping Tina wasn't watching her from up there.

"They're... yes..." Rosamund had the phone up in front of her face.

"What?" Annie snapped. *That's my bloody phone, you know.* "What can you see?"

"It's a man. They're shifting him from..." Rosamund lowered the phone. Her face was pale.

"What?" Annie grabbed for the phone, catching it just before her friend dropped it.

Rosamund stared towards the Cobb, her mouth open. "It's..."

"What?" Annie said. She pulled up her phone, but whatever they'd pulled out of the water was obscured by two uniformed officers.

Dougie was one of them.

"I think we should get back," she said.

Rosamund nodded, mute. She looked at Annie, her expression blank.

Annie put a hand on her arm. "You OK, Rosamund?"

Another nod. "I need to..."

"What? What d'you need to do? You look like you've seen a ghost."

Rosamund gave a small gasp. Annie looked back towards the Cobb. Tim was approaching, waving an arm.

"Ah, hell," she muttered. "Come on, Rosamund."

She turned to grab her friend's arm, to guide her back towards the town. She'd take her into the Cobb Arms, get her a stiff drink.

But Rosamund was gone.

CHAPTER FIVE

LESLEY STOOD as her team filed into her office. Strictly speaking, just half of her team. She didn't often get them all in here anymore. And she still wasn't sure how she felt about managing two teams instead of one.

Sure, in Birmingham she'd managed more than two teams, sometimes as many as four. But she'd been sent here to Dorset specifically to reduce her workload. The idea was to get a bit of peace and quiet and recover from the PTSD she'd suffered after a bomb attack in Birmingham. A string of murders and the investigation into the death of her predecessor, DCI Mackie, had put paid to that peace and quiet, but at least she hadn't had multiple teams to manage.

Until now.

The people sitting in front of her were the Cold Cases Team, not the Major Crimes Investigation Team she'd led until the super had decided to give her more responsibility. It made sense; a DCI wasn't really supposed to head up a single investigation team.

And now they had a DI for her old team. Not that she was here yet.

But her new DI for cold cases was very much here, and she looked raring to go. DI Jill Scott perched on the edge of the chair in front of Lesley's desk. If this had been her old office, the one with those goddamn glass windows looking out over the car park, Lesley would have thought of Dennis.

She wasn't letting herself think about Dennis.

The team's three DCs, Mike, Stanley and Katie, were hovering behind their new boss. Katie was chewing a pen, looking like she might blurt something out at any moment. Stanley was standing with his shoulders hunched, looking tired. Mike was eyeing Jill.

Mike didn't like not having Dennis here.

But people retired, and the world continued. He'd just have to get used to it.

"Sit down everybody," Lesley said. "We haven't got long. You need to get on the road."

"Who does?" asked Mike, taking a seat at the back.

This room was smaller than her old office, and square. There was a window, but it was to the side, not behind her. And mercifully, it had blinds.

Lesley looked at Mike. He wasn't her most brilliant team member, but he was steady, all the more so since he'd married Tina. He could be relied on to do as he was told, knocking on doors, interviewing suspects, trawling through evidence. He had the occasional flash of brilliance, but she wasn't sure he didn't actually steal most of those from his wife.

Stanley and Katie took two of the remaining seats. Lesley's desk was more of a table, and the seats were gathered around it. Jill turned to one side and then the other, giving her new team encouraging smiles. Lesley wondered what she'd done so far to foster team spirit. Well, now she had her chance.

"OK," she said. "Can someone close the door?"

Katie jumped up and pushed the door shut, causing the advent calendar hanging on it to slam against the wood. This was Lesley's sole concession to the festive season, and something her wife Elsa had given her. It was practical; a tiny chocolate bar behind every door.

"Boss." Jill leaned forward. "I've spoken to PS Hinton in Lyme, asked him to fill me in."

Lesley raised an eyebrow. *Good.* "OK. What did he tell you?"

Jill opened her notebook. "Two divers were working on the Cobb this morning. Seems they were doing repairs to the fabric of the—"

"Yes, yes," Lesley said. "They found the body, yes?"

Jill flushed. "Yes, boss. A man. In a pretty bad way, but he was wearing an orange coat, or the remains of one, so we're hoping to identify him from that."

"Surely orange coats are pretty common?" Stanley pointed out.

Jill shrugged. "We'll need to see the body, obviously. But it's a man, and there's no immediate sign of what killed him."

"Not drowning?" Katie asked.

Jill turned to look at her. "We can't make any assumptions. Especially not with the body in the state it's in. One leg and half an arm are missing, probably eaten by wildlife. But I'm told there's no damage that isn't consistent with its being in the sea for a while."

"How long had he been there?" Stanley asked. Mike was narrowing his eyes, tapping his chin.

"They haven't established that yet," Jill said. "A few years, is the current thinking."

"What's on your mind, Mike?" Lesley asked.

He looked up. "Oh, nothing."

"Tina's on leave for a couple of days. She over there?"

He nodded.

"Have you spoken to her?"

Jill looked puzzled. "I'm sorry. Tina? Tina Abbott?"

Lesley gave her a smile. "She's Mike's wife."

"Oh. I didn't know that."

Mike flashed a smile at his new boss. "All the best people have a wife in the MCIT."

Jill looked down, and Lesley thought of Meera. A good officer, who'd been instrumental when they'd had to swell the ranks of the MCIT's previous iteration.

"So," Lesley said, clapping her hands together. "We've got a man, no idea how long he's been in the water, but a fair while, judging by what we've got." She turned her gaze on Jill. "The first case for your new team."

Jill nodded and straightened up. "We need to get over there."

"You do," Lesley agreed. "Mike, we all know what Lyme's like. Any inside information from Tina?"

Another grin. "Her mum's down at the harbour with her mates, watching."

"Her mates?" Lesley asked.

Mike shook his head. "You don't want to know about Annie's mates."

Lesley had met Annie Abbott before. She'd stayed in the woman's spare room when they'd been investigating two bodies that had been uncovered following a landslip along from Lyme Regis beach. She could well imagine what Annie's mates would be like.

"So that's all she's told you?" she said.

"Sorry, boss."

Lesley nodded. If Mike was getting his information from a member of the public, she'd prefer if that information was incomplete for now.

"Right," she said. "Time to head over there."

She was about to turn to Jill when the DI raised her hand. Lesley gave her a smile. "This isn't school, Jill."

"Sorry, boss. So it's definitely a cold case?"

"That's what the super's saying," Lesley said. "A body left in water does decompose slower. The damage we've been told about would be consistent with much more recent death if he'd been found in the open. But it can take years for a body to decompose in water."

Jill grimaced. "Right." She made a note in her notepad.

"We don't know much yet," Lesley added. "Hopefully we will, once the pathologist and forensics have reported. Might even give us an ID."

"It's probably somebody who fell off the harbour wall," said Mike. "It can get pretty slippy on the Cobb."

Lesley looked at him. "You visit a lot?"

He shrugged. "A bit. Not doing Christmas this year. T's not looking forward to Annie's reaction when we tell her."

Lesley smiled. As always, she and Elsa would have Sharon with them for Christmas. Her ex, Terry, liked to go travelling with his new family. She glanced out through the glazed door; decorations adorned the desks, a small tree on Tina's desk and what looked like some kind of picture of Santa Claus, painted by Louis.

"Right." She stood up. "I need two of you at least over there. Jill, it's your shout."

Jill nodded. "Mike, you've got the local knowledge. You and I will go."

"What about me?" asked Stanley.

Jill failed to stifle a roll of the eyes, visible only from Lesley's direction. Lesley snorted.

"You and Katie stay here and collate evidence," the DI said. "Start by finding out if there are any historical reports of missing people in the area. Start two years back."

"Two years?" Stanley asked. "Until when?"

A shrug. "Until you find enough to give us some leads. And Katie, I want you to talk to local police. Make sure we know as soon as they get an ID. If they get an ID."

"Yes, boss."

"Call me guv." Jill gestured towards Lesley. "The DCI's the boss."

"Yes, guv."

Lesley smiled. It was good to see Jill using her initiative, but then, she *was* a DI. Her previous second-in-command had been a sergeant: DS Dennis Frampton. He was retired, but still in contact with members of the team.

"Report back to me when you're there," she told Jill.

"Yes, boss."

"Good. Hopefully we'll get this wrapped up—"

"In time for Christmas?" Stanley asked with a smile.

Christmas was just over a week away.

"Let's see what we can do, eh, Stanley? But no cutting corners."

CHAPTER SIX

TINA SAT at her mum's kitchen table, clutching a cup of tea. The house felt empty, without Louis in it. Should she feel guilty for enjoying the peace and quiet without him?

Sure, Annie was a help. More than a help. She'd have bent over backwards to look after Louis at every available opportunity. But the fact was, Tina lived in Sandford outside Wareham and Annie lived in Lyme Regis, over an hour's drive away. So her mum wasn't often available for childcare assistance.

She leaned back and closed her eyes. Somewhere out the back window, seagulls cawed. The constant backdrop to life in Lyme Regis.

Tina was a DC, hoping to become a DS at some point. Mike pulled his weight, but his job was high stress, too.

The reality was, she found it hard. And now there was another one due in four months, and it was only going to get harder.

She stroked her stomach, which had been churning all

the way back up the hill from the Cobb. She'd started showing much earlier with this one than with Louis, and she knew her colleagues were uneasy working with a pregnant DC again.

Well, tough.

Right now, she was getting a welcome few moments to herself. She'd left the Cobb not long after arriving, told in no uncertain terms by the local police that she was off duty and not needed. There'd been glances towards her bump, too. Pretty rich, she thought; she was a DC in the MCIT. What did they know? But she couldn't argue with the off-duty bit.

She'd walked back through the town, hoping to bump into Annie on her way but finding the house empty when she'd arrived. *Take the small mercies when you can get them.* She just hoped Louis was OK.

She heard the front door crash open and straightened up, opening her eyes. She took a few deep breaths. The moments of silence were over.

The kitchen door was flung open. Annie hurtled in, followed by her friend, Rosamund. Rosamund had been a friend of Annie's for the last year or two, since they'd both taken up regular swimming in the bay. She was quiet and sometimes standoffish. Snooty, Mike reckoned. Tina was hoping that eventually she'd locate the woman's softer side.

"Tina," Annie said, throwing herself into a chair. "Do you know anything about what's happened up at the Cobb?"

Tina eyed her mum. "Where's Louis?"

Annie bit her lip. "Oh, sorry love. He's in his pushchair in the hall. You know I can't get it in here."

Tina nodded. "Asleep?"

"Not far off waking up."

Tina slumped into her chair. Waking up from a nap at this time of day meant Louis would be grumpy. And she was tired. She yawned.

"So?" said Annie. "What have they told you? We saw a man."

Tina sighed. This was her mum all over. She knew everyone in this town, and she made it her business to know their business, too. People in Lyme Regis were used to it; they did it themselves. But this was different.

"I can't tell you, Mum. You know that."

Annie's lips tightened. She was sitting opposite Tina, her hands on the table, fingers splayed out. Her eyes were wide, searching Tina's face as if expecting to find information there and pull it out by sheer force of will. Tina glanced up at Rosamund. She was leaning against the wall, her face pale.

"You OK, Rosamund?" Tina asked. The woman ignored her.

"She's been like that ever since we spotted him," Annie said, glancing up at her friend.

"Spotted who?" Tina asked.

"The body."

Tina looked towards the kitchen door. "Close that, will you?"

Annie sighed and heaved herself up from her chair. She closed the door, heaving herself back like Tina had made her walk ten miles.

"What is it, Mum?" Tina said. "What did you spot?"

"They pulled someone out of the harbour at the end of the Cobb."

Tina nodded. She'd been there. "I know. But the area was cordoned off. You shouldn't—"

"Rosamund knows him."

Tina was about to speak when her phone rang: Mike. She picked up, holding the phone to her ear as she watched her mum's face, occasionally glancing over at Rosamund, still leaning against the wall. Rosamund was always pale; her short blonde hair framed a light, waif-like face. But right now, she looked like she might faint at any moment.

"Mike," Tina said, "we're in the middle of something now."

"Is it the body they've found in the harbour?"

She swallowed. "Yes. Have they put you on it?"

"He's been there a while. Maybe years. So yes, it's been decreed a cold case."

Tina grunted. She glanced at Rosamund again. She needed to speak to the woman.

But if this was a cold case, the MCIT, the team she belonged to, would have nothing to do with it.

"Are you coming over here?" she asked her husband.

"That's why I'm calling. Can your mum put me up tonight and tomorrow, too?"

"Of course." Tina put her hand over the microphone. "Mum. Mike's being sent here for work. Can he...?"

"Course, love." Annie smiled. She stood up and went to the kettle, which she filled and clicked on with a flourish. Rosamund stayed leaning against the wall, muttering now.

"I've just come out of a briefing with the DCI," Mike said. "Jill and I are heading over your way."

"Jill?" Tina said.

"It's OK," he told her. "She lives in Dorchester. She won't be staying in your mum's spare room."

Tina smiled. Having the DCI here had been challenging. And she didn't know DI Scott at all.

Annie leaned towards Tina and grabbed her hand. "What's going on, Tina? What's he saying?"

Tina shook her mum's hand off. "Wait," she mouthed. Annie slumped back into in her chair.

Tina gestured towards Rosamund, indicating that Annie should help her friend sit down. Maybe give her a cup of tea.

Annie frowned back at her daughter, then stood up, looking reluctant. She put an arm around Rosamund and guided her into a chair. Rosamund sat, her eyes blank, her gaze straight ahead.

What's wrong with her?

"OK," Tina said, her gaze on Rosamund. "Do you have an ID?"

Tina had grown up in Lyme Regis. She knew half the people here. She clenched her fist as she waited for an answer. Rosamund's expression hadn't changed.

"No idea yet," Mike said. "We're hoping to get one soon, though."

Tina considered. "You might want to talk to my mum's friend."

"Sorry? Why?"

Tina looked at Rosamund. She'd seen the state the body was in. How could she possibly...?

"It's... I'll tell you when you get here."

Annie was leaning on Rosamund now, making soothing noises. From the hallway, Tina heard the sound of Louis waking. Low grumbles, which would swiftly turn into a cry if she didn't do something.

"I've got to go, love," she said. "I know you'll go straight to the scene, but tell me when you get here, yes?"

"Of course. Love you."

"Love you."

She put the phone down and stood, heading for her son in the hall. As she passed Rosamund's chair, the woman turned and grabbed her wrist.

Tina looked back. Rosamund was staring up at her.

"I know," she said.

Tina exchanged a glance with Annie, who nodded.

Rosamund's gaze on her intensified. "I know who it is."

CHAPTER SEVEN

MIKE DROPPED the phone into his lap.

DI Scott was driving. They were on the A35, approaching the familiar turnoff for Lyme Regis.

He liked the new DI. She hadn't been his boss for long, but in that time, she'd shown respect for his experience and his knowledge of the local patch. She'd sat down with him on her first day and asked him to talk her through the cases he'd worked on over the last few years, including the investigation into DCI Mackie's death.

He'd been reluctant to talk about that one, given the sarge's involvement, but she seemed trustworthy enough, and eventually he'd opened up. He hoped he'd made the right decision.

"Was that Tina?" she asked, glancing at his phone, then in the rear-view mirror before taking the roundabout and the A3052.

He nodded. "She's at her mum's house. I was supposed to be going over there tomorrow to show Louis the Christmas lights."

"Are they nice? The lights in Lyme Regis, I mean."

Mike shrugged. "Tasteful. All white. Christmas trees with special mounts over the shop windows. I reckon there must be some sort of edict: 'Don't put coloured lights on your Christmas trees, on pain of death.'"

The guv laughed. "Lyme Regis is that kind of place."

He wondered how often she'd been here. That accent wasn't local. "The pleasure gardens are a bit more colourful," he said. "They light the trees up in multi-colours. Louis loved it last year."

She nodded. DI Scott had a little girl with her wife, Meera, who Mike had worked with. He wasn't sure how old the girl was, but he didn't like to pry.

What would it be like next year? With Louis and a younger sibling, too?

"Tina grew up in Lyme Regis?" the DI asked.

He nodded. "Her mum, Annie, still lives in the same house Tina grew up in on Anning Road."

"Anning Road? After Mary Ann—"

"Mary Anning, yes. She's a local legend."

"I know." Her cheeks reddened. "I saw the film."

He'd seen it, too. *Ammonite.* It hadn't been what he'd expected.

"Annie knows everybody," he said, "so she'll be useful, hopefully. Mind you, I'm not sure how much of what Annie says is true and how much is confabulation."

The DI nodded. "I had an aunt like that."

Had. She didn't have a Dorset accent. Mike wondered where her family came from. Meera had talked about her own parents, but never mentioned her wife's.

"So," he said, "have you been told any more about an ID?"

"Not yet," the guv replied.

"Tina said something about Annie's friend knowing who it is. But I'm not sure how reliable she'll be."

A nod. "We'll talk to her, see what she has to say."

Mike knew what she was thinking; with a body in the water that long, how could anyone recognise him?

His phone buzzed. A message from Tina: *Rosamund still says she knows who it is. Won't tell us.*

"Shit."

The DI pipped the brakes as they approached a bend. The sea filled the view to their left. "What's up?" she said.

"Rosamund, that's Tina's mum's mate. She's not saying anything."

"Any reason why not?"

He shrugged and tapped out a message. *Why won't she tell you? ID would be useful.* But Tina knew that.

He waited for a response as they hit the edge of Lyme Regis.

"Which way to the Cobb?" she asked.

"Keep going straight. Through town and then you'll need to take a left turn."

She nodded and slowed for a car to pass them on the narrow street.

His phone buzzed.

She's sitting at Mum's kitchen table sobbing. I've never seen Rosamund sob.

Mike looked at his boss. "She seems a bit overcome by it all."

"Who?"

"Rosamund. The witness."

"We'll speak to her after we've seen the body, identified anyone else who might be hanging around." The guv turned to him. "If someone in that town is responsible, they'll want to keep an eye on us."

"I know." Problem was, everyone in Lyme kept an eye on everyone else at the best of times.

"Who else does Tina know?" the DI asked. "Any other mates of her mum's who might be helpful? Could this Rosamund be involved somehow?"

He shrugged. He'd never met Rosamund, or any of Annie's swimming friends, although he'd heard enough about them. He'd seen Annie come in from her morning dip a few times, shivering as she brought the cold air into the kitchen. Why anyone would want to do that at that time of day was beyond him.

Rosamund. He tried to place her. Was she the eccentric one with the shop on Broad Street, or the stuffy one who lived in the mansion just back from the town centre? He was pretty sure it wasn't the young one who lived in the caravan on the beach.

"Sorry, guv," he said. "I'm not sure. D'you want me to call Tina back?"

"Not yet," she told him. "Let's go to your mother-in-law's house. See what we can find out."

"I thought we were heading for the Cobb?" They'd already passed the turnoff for Anning Road.

She wrinkled her nose. "True. OK. I'll drop you at the Cobb. You liaise with forensics and pathology if they're there, find out what we know so far. I'll go to Annie's house. Message me with her address."

"Isn't it better for me to do that?" he asked.

She shook her head. "You're too close to it. Let's keep it professional."

Mike nodded. *Keep it professional.* So the trust only went so far.

CHAPTER EIGHT

THERE WAS a squad car blocking their entrance to the harbour. The DI pulled up and showed her ID.

The PC dipped down to look inside and gave Mike a nod. "Alright, mate."

"Good to see you, Dougie," said Mike.

"You know him?" asked the guv.

"PC Douglas Anderson. He's married to Tina's sister," Mike explained.

Dougie peered past Mike at the DI. "Evening, ma'am."

She smiled and nodded at him. "Even more incestuous here than I thought," Jill said with a smile as she closed the window. "I'm going to drop you here. Don't get too pally with the locals, eh?"

He nodded and opened the car door.

As he did so, the movement of the wing mirror gave him a view of the road coming down to the harbour. Tina was there, hurrying down with her mum. She was struggling to stop Louis's pushchair from rolling down the hill in front of them.

He felt his jaw clench.

Tina was on leave, spending time with her mum before Christmas, getting some well-needed rest.

Mike bent to look at the DI in the driver's seat. "Change of plan," he told her.

"How so?" She had her hands on the steering wheel, impatient to be off.

"Tina and her mum are here."

She turned in her seat. "What about the friend?"

He shrugged. "I'll ask."

"No." She put a hand on his shoulder. "I'll ask."

Mike gave her a nod. "I'll head along the Cobb. Take a look at what's going on."

"Good thinking."

"I'll explain to your wife that it's my decision, not yours."

He left the car, giving Tina a wave as he headed away towards the Cobb.

"You alright, Mike?" Dougie said as he passed the cordon. "You got here quick."

He shrugged. "New boss is a good driver."

Dougie looked up the hill to where Jill was hurrying towards Tina and Annie.

"What's she like? Better than your old boss?"

Mike wrinkled his nose, thinking of the sarge. Truth was, DS Frampton had always favoured Johnny. Even after Johnny had left for the Met.

"Different," he said.

Dennis had been as old-school as they came, but he was decent, and Mike and he had built a relationship of sorts over the years. He'd never been the sarge's favourite, but he'd known the sarge trusted him.

Now he was reporting directly to a DI, and it felt different. Like he had to prove himself all over again. Still, Jill seemed fair.

He gave Dougie a smile. *No need to tell him all that.* "Will I be disturbing anything if I walk along to the end of the Cobb?" he asked.

"Nah, mate. They pulled the body out of the water this morning. He went in a long time ago, there's not much to disturb."

Mike looked towards the point where the Cobb forked. A forensic tent had already been set up and was billowing in the wind. Two white-suited figures moved around outside it.

He wondered if one of them was Gail Hansford. She'd have done well to get all the way over here from Swanage already, but then Gail was like that.

"Who are the techs?" he asked.

"Not sure," Dougie replied. "I haven't been up there."

"Fair enough." Mike gave his brother-in-law a friendly clap on the shoulder. "See you in a bit."

"No problem, mate."

Mike walked along the Cobb, pulling his coat tighter around him. It was just days to go until Christmas, and bloody freezing out here. In particularly rough weather, the Cobb would get closed off. There were no barriers to stop people climbing to its upper level, and nothing to stop them falling off into the sea. But still, people insisted on climbing the sloping steps to the top so they could get a view or do their own impression of Meryl Streep in *The French Lieu-tenant's Woman.*

Mike wasn't about to take the upper route.

He strode along the bottom level, masts on the boats in the harbour clanging beside him.

The wind wasn't all that high for this time of year, but he

could still feel it whistling around his ears. It was like there was a line halfway up his head at the point where the harbour wall sheltered him.

He shivered. He still couldn't get his head round what it must have been like for Tina growing up here. It was so different from where he'd grown up in Poole. There were harbours, and there were harbours.

As he approached the forensic tent, one of the white-suited figures peeled away and walked towards him. It removed its hood and gave him a smile.

"Gail," he said. "You got here fast."

"My little van can go faster than you think." She pulled down her mask and grinned. "You're here with Tina?"

He shook his head. "The new DI." He pointed back towards the town. "She's up there now interviewing poten-tial witnesses."

Gail raised an eyebrow. "We got any?"

"There's a friend of Tina's mum who might have known the dead guy. Have you got an ID yet?"

"Nope. Nothing in his pockets, or what's left of them, no tattoos, no identifying marks. And he's... well, let's say he's been in the water a very long time. But there's only so much interrogation of the body that we can do along here, and besides, pathology have told us it's not worth their while coming out. Not with a cold case."

"Who will it be? Doing the post-mortem?"

She shrugged. "Probably the guy from Exeter."

That made sense. Exeter might have been in Devon, but it was closer to Lyme Regis than Poole or Dorchester.

"You're going to let me take a look then?" Mike asked.

"Be my guest." Gail turned away from him and started

walking to the forensic tent. "You brought a protective suit?" she asked.

He stopped. *Shit.* If he'd been in his own car, he'd have had one in the boot, but he'd never thought to ask the DI.

She laughed. "Don't worry, Mike, I've got one you can use."

He swallowed. "Thanks."

"Come on, then," she told him. "Time for you to take a look at this body."

CHAPTER NINE

JILL CAST a smile in the direction of DC Abbott and her mum as she climbed the hill towards them. Everywhere here was hills, narrow lanes, and locals who all seemed to know each other. This was the first death she'd been sent to investigate since joining her new team, and she hadn't expected to be plunged into the middle of a family dynamic as well. She forced a smile as Tina and Annie approached; no need for them to know about her nerves.

"Tina," she said.

"Good to see you, ma'am." Tina gave her a nod.

Annie was frowning. "You've pulled a body out?" she said, looking past Jill.

Jill resisted a glance backwards. "A man was found in the harbour early this morning," she replied, "he'd been dead for some time. I believe—"

"Do we have an ID yet?" Tina asked.

"Rosamund says she knows who he is," Annie added. "My friend, Rosamund."

Jill nodded. It was this Rosamund she really needed to be speaking to. "Has she given you a name?"

Annie grunted. She had hold of a McLaren buggy, the same sort Jill and Meera had bought for Suzi, but in black. Inside it was a boy of two or three; Tina's son, she assumed. Annie was pushing the pushchair back and forth, rocking it absentmindedly.

"Not yet," she said. "She's... she's come over all weird."

The boy squawked and Tina bent to pat his hand, making Jill wonder what Meera and Suzi were doing. Suzi was two and a half, a similar age to Tina's boy. She'd be having tea, being read a story, getting settled for bed.

Her chest tightened. She'd only been out here a few hours, and already she missed them.

"OK," she said. "So, where's your friend? Have you left her at your house?"

Annie hoiked her thumb backwards, up the hill. "She's in the pub."

"The pub."

Tina was looking down at the ground. Was she embarrassed by her own mum?

"Nag's Head," Annie said. "Reckon she needed a drink."

"Right," Jill said. "Can you take me to her? Will there be somewhere private in there I can speak to her?"

"I'll have a word with Eddie. He works behind the bar." She gave Jill a wink. "Don't worry, I'll sort it."

The older woman turned away and hurried up the hill. Jill was impressed by her fitness, but then, living in a town like Lyme Regis, you'd get used to walking up hills fast.

She hung back, grabbing an opportunity to speak to Tina, who was now pushing the pushchair. The boy was fast asleep.

"Is there any information you can give me on this witness?" she asked the DC.

"Rosamund?" Tina asked.

Jill nodded. *Yes, Rosamund.* Did being in Lyme Regis slow Tina's brain? Or was it the effect of being with her son?

Tina shrugged. "She's a friend of my mum's, has been for a couple of years, I think. I don't know her all that well. They met through the swimming club. There's this group of women. They meet every morning, swim down at the harbour not too far from... You don't need to know all that."

Jill gave her a smile. "And this Rosamund, she says she knows the man. Do you think she might be involved?" Jill asked.

"Involved? Rosamund?"

Jill gave another nod. They were nearing the top of Cobb Road, an open space to their right and a car park to the left. Annie was crossing the car park, unencumbered by the pushchair and the dead weight of a sleeping child. Warm light spilled from the windows of cottages and houses, with more Christmas trees in the windows than Jill was used to seeing at home. She shivered, realising how cold she was.

"I don't think she'd be involved," Tina said. "Rosamund, well, she can be a bit standoffish sometimes, and she looked bloody pale. Sorry. Very pale, when she was in Mum's kitchen. But I don't think she's a suspect."

Jill eyed the DC. "Are you just saying that because she's your mum's friend?"

Tina gave her a wary smile and shook her head. "Do you want me to sit in?"

The last thing Jill needed was an officer not even from her team, related indirectly to a witness and possibly to the victim. She was concerned enough about having Mike here.

"Thanks, Tina," she said, "but you're on leave. I'll be fine as I am."

Tina looked disappointed. "OK, but, well, I'll hang around, keep Mum company. Let me know if you need me."

"I will." Jill looked down at the pushchair. "Shouldn't you be getting home with your son?"

Tina followed Jill's eyes down and smiled. "He's asleep now. He'll be fine. Mum needs me more than he does."

Jill raised an eyebrow. From what she'd seen of Annie Abbott, she strongly doubted that. "Up to you. Thanks, Tina."

They'd taken a sharp right turn now and were at last heading downhill. The pub was on the left, right up against the pavement. She pushed open the door and strode in, pausing to let Tina pass through with the buggy, but then advancing to make it clear she didn't need Tina to accompany her. Annie was standing at the bar chatting to an elderly man who leaned against it.

"This is Eddie," Annie said. "He's already put Rosamund in a bedroom. They don't have a snug or anything here."

"Thanks," Jill said to the man. She put a hand in her pocket for her ID. "My name's—"

He waved a hand in dismissal. "Aye, aye. Annie here's told me everything. You're DI Jill Scott, Dorset Cold Cases Team. You work with our Tina over there."

Our Tina. Was this yet another person related to DC Abbott? Jill glanced round to see Tina smiling.

"I'm not 'our' anyone, Eddie," she said. "Don't mind him, boss."

Jill narrowed her eyes. She wasn't Tina's boss.

"Thanks," she said to the man. The sooner she got into a

private room with the witness, the better. "Can you show me where I can speak to Rosamund, please?"

"Course I can, love," he told her. "Come with me."

.

CHAPTER TEN

JILL FOLLOWED Eddie up the stairs to a room immediately above the bar. Eddie knocked lightly on the door and then opened it after a response Jill didn't even hear.

The witness was sitting on the bed in a small, neatly furnished bedroom. She was in her mid-fifties, younger than Annie, with mid-length mousy hair pushed behind her ears. She sat on the end of the bed, twitching every now and then. Was that nerves or some sort of tic?

Jill cleared her throat, and the woman looked up.

"You must be Rosamund," she said.

The woman's eyes widened. She looked Jill up and down, slowly. "And you must be Tina's new boss."

Jill shook her head, taking a seat opposite Rosamund at a pale dressing table. "Not Tina's new boss. Mike's. Her husband."

Rosamund smiled. "He's a good boy, that one. Slightly slow occasionally, but he's been good for Tina."

Jill nodded. She wasn't here to learn about Tina and

Mike's family life. "I gather you've lived in Lyme for some time," she said.

A nod. "I live on Ware Lane, just under a mile up the hill." She hooked her finger towards the window. "I've known Annie for... thirteen months now."

Very precise, thought Jill. "The man who was pulled out of the water in the harbour this morning. I'm told that you know who he is."

Rosamund's gaze dropped to her lap. "I do."

"And can you share it with me?"

Rosamund swallowed. She dragged her head up to look into Jill's face. Her own face was ashen. "You think I'm a suspect, don't you? They always think that."

Jill shook her head. "All we know right now is that you know who the man is. It would be very helpful if you told me."

"Yes. I... his name's Roger. Was. Roger Gallagher."

"And how do you know him?"

"He's a friend of my husband. Golfing friend. You know the kind of thing."

Jill didn't. "Your husband?"

"My..." The woman's gaze dropped again. "Yes, well, he was... they used to play golf together."

"And they don't now?"

"Not recently. Not for... Well, not for a while."

Rosamund was tugging her fingernail. Lifting her finger off her lap repeatedly, and then letting it flick back down again.

"How well did *you* know Roger?" Jill asked.

A shrug. "Not that well."

"When might be the last time you saw him?"

Rosamund sucked her teeth. "I..." She looked up. "Let

me think." She closed her eyes. "Four years, just under. It was Christmas."

"Would your husband have seen him more recently?"

Rosamund shook her head. "No, definitely not."

Jill leaned in. "So was Roger local?"

Another nod. "Charmouth. He has – *had* – a house just outside Charmouth. Nice place, apparently. Sea views."

"Any family?"

Another shrug. "Sorry. I don't know."

"So you last saw him four years ago. Did you hear talk that he'd gone missing? Did your husband say anything?"

If it was possible, Rosamund seemed to have gone even paler. "No. Sorry. No."

"Do you know where he worked? If he worked?"

"He... well, he was retired. I can tell you that, otherwise he wouldn't have been playing golf with my husband on Tuesday afternoons. Some sort of property business, I think. Ran it himself. Sorry, that's all I know. I only met him a few times."

Jill eyed the woman. If Roger was somebody she'd only had a passing acquaintance with, then why did she look so scared?

"So this business of Mr Gallagher," Jill said. "Was it based in Charmouth, Lyme Regis, Axminster?"

"I can't tell you that either, I'm afraid. He sold it before I met him." She licked her lips. "Sorry. I don't know any more than that."

There was a glass on the table next to the bed. Rosamund swirled it around. "I need another glass of water."

Jill wondered what had happened to the drink Annie had bought for her friend. The two of them seemed to have different ideas of the best way to deal with shock.

"I'm sure we can manage that," Jill said. She needed to report back to her team anyway. The sooner they had the victim's name, the sooner they could start tracking down his family. Inform his next of kin.

She stood up, holding the glass. It smelled of whisky. *So that explains it.*

"I'll need your address, Mrs..."

"Winters," Rosamund said. "Rosamund Winters. I'll let you have my address." She slumped. "You'll be wanting to come to the house, talk to my husband."

At no point had she suggested that Jill might want to speak to Mr Winters.

Was that suspicious, or was it just Lyme Regis?

CHAPTER ELEVEN

"You go home, Mum," Tina said. "No point in you staying out here in this cold."

"Oh, don't mollycoddle me like that," her mum replied. "I'm not as old as you seem to think. And besides, it isn't cold in here."

They were still in the Nag's Head. Rosamund was presumably still upstairs with the DI. And the truth was, it *was* cold in here. Every time the door opened, it brought a blast of freezing air that assaulted the senses.

Tina resisted a roll of her eyes. Her mum was only in her early fifties, but she hadn't thought to put a coat on before she'd come out.

"I'm dying for a cuppa," she said. "You go home and put the kettle on. I'll be right with you."

"What are you going to do?"

Tina rocked the pushchair back and forth. Louis was still out for the count. She knew this was a bad idea. He'd wake when she put him to bed, and then she'd regret it.

"I just need to check in with Mike," she told her mum. "He's down at the harbour."

"Okay, hun," her mum said. "Don't be too long."

"Yeah."

She gave Tina's shoulder a squeeze and leaned in for a hug. Tina returned it. Her mum could be overbearing, sometimes irritating, but she cared, and she adored Louis.

"Tell you what," Annie said, "forget the cuppa. I'll go down to the Kiosk and pick up a coffee."

"There's no way they'll be open now." *And besides, that's all the way back down at the beach.* But Annie didn't want to miss out.

Annie looked at her watch. "What happened to the time?" She sighed. "You're right, I'll go home. See you in a bit."

Tina gave her a tight smile and waved her off. Annie strode off towards Sherborne Lane and the steep cut-through towards her house. Tina was always impressed with her mum's level of fitness. Living her entire life in Lyme Regis meant she was practised in steaming up and down hills, and Annie never moved slowly.

Tina walked along Pound Street and back down Cobb Road to the harbour, anxious not to go too fast in case the pushchair built up too much momentum. Pushing it had been getting harder as her bump enlarged.

Mike was just leaving the harbour wall as she approached, making for a car she didn't recognise. She guessed it must be the DI's.

"Hey T," he said, spotting her.

She wheeled the pushchair down and waited for him to bend down and give Louis a stroke on the face. Louis didn't stir.

"How's it going?" she asked him. "Is it suspicious?"

He gave her a wink. "Always on duty, DC Tina Abbott."

She laughed. "Well, they pulled a body out of the water only a couple of miles away from my mum's house. Of course I want to know what's going on."

He raised an eyebrow. "Now, the only reason—"

"Yes," she told him, avoiding his gaze. "We both know you're on the Cold Cases Team now."

He nodded. They both knew this wasn't her case But they also both knew it didn't always work like that. She'd helped him when she was on maternity leave and Trevor Hamm's body had turned up at Blue Pool, after all.

She pushed aside the trouble they'd both got into for that.

"Anyway," she said. "This body. Is it suspicious?"

He looked at her. "You'll know as much as I do. Doesn't your mum know who it is?"

She shook her head. "Her mate Rosamund does, but—"

Mike's phone rang. Tina watched as he pulled it out of the pocket of his coat, nodding. "Guv. Right, thanks. I'll let Stan know he can start doing some research behind the scenes in the office. Of course. Thanks."

He hung up.

"Man of many words," Tina said to him.

"Don't you start."

"So," she said, "what was that about?"

"Your mum's mate Rosamund has coughed," he told her. "Roger Gallagher, old golfing friend of her husband. She hasn't seen him for almost four years."

Tina nodded. Relationships in Lyme Regis were like that, a string of people who all knew each other. It was like the six degrees of separation game, all in one Dorset town.

"Anything else?" she asked.

He shook his head. "Pathologist isn't prioritising the PM. Forensics say there's very little to be found, with him having been in the water so long."

"How long?"

"For it to be a cold case, it'll be three years. Which fits with what Rosamund has said."

"Yeah. What was his name again?"

"Roger Gallagher."

She frowned as she tried to place the name, but it wasn't familiar.

"Have they removed the body?"

Mike nodded. "He's gone to Exeter."

"Exeter?" Last time they'd covered a case in Lyme Regis, they'd ended up dealing with the authorities in Exeter. It hadn't gone smoothly.

"I know," he said. "But the DCI doesn't know yet. And your new boss... well, she won't be getting involved anyway."

"No."

"Look, T, there's not much to do now. We might as well go home."

"You mean my mum's."

"Yeah." He didn't look too happy about it. She pushed back her irritation and put her hand over his on the handle of the pushchair.

The baby was kicking. *Best to get into the warm.* "It's nice to have you here early."

"I'm working, remember. I might have to go back to Winfrith at short notice."

As they turned back up the hill she leaned into him. "I know."

"And, T?"

"Yes?"

"This isn't your case, right? Let me and the DI handle it."

CHAPTER TWELVE

If DC Katie Young had knocked on Lesley's door once, she'd done it a hundred times. Sure, it was always to update her on progress. But did she really need to report every fifteen minutes?

Lesley sighed at another knock.

"Ma'am," Katie said.

Lesley gritted her teeth. "Boss will do."

Katie flushed. "Sorry, boss. I've still got nothing on him disappearing yet." A shrug. "Nothing on police records, nothing on Google. I've been trying social media but..." A shrug. "I have made some progress, though."

"Which is?"

"A wife. Widow. Sophie. She lives at the same address he was last at."

"And she never reported him missing?"

"Not to the police."

Lesley chewed her bottom lip. If Roger Gallagher had been missing for four years, and his wife had never said anything...

It was odd. It was more than odd.

"Name of Sophie West," Katie said. "Reverted to her maiden name, by the looks of it. Or kept the name all along."

"We need to speak to her. Before she hears the news from somewhere else," Lesley said.

"She's wealthy," Katie replied. "The house is just outside Charmouth. Sea views. Big."

"Kids?"

"Not sure."

"Well, see what you can get. How's Stanley getting on?"

"He's still looking for anything about Roger disappearing. I'll focus on the family, if that's..."

"Fine." Lesley considered. "You contact the DI. Tell her what you've found. She and Mike need to get over there."

Katie pulled her shoulders back. "Already done it, boss."

"Good. Well, report back to me when we have more."

"Yes, ma-a... boss." Katie backed out of the office and closed the door.

It was almost seven. Yes, there was a murder case on, but Lesley wasn't SIO. Elsa would be wondering where she was. And there was bound to be house move admin to do.

Which, if she was honest with herself, was one of the reasons she was still here.

She grabbed her keys from the desk and left the room. Passing Katie and Stanley, she gave them a nod. "Don't stay too late."

"The guv and Mike are going to speak to Sophie West," Katie said. Do you want me to update y—"

"No," Lesley said. She had to let them do their job. "But you two go home as soon as you've finished what you're doing right now. We'll reconvene in the morning."

Stanley looked up and nodded. Katie looked as if she might be about to argue, then thought better of it.

"Charmouth," Lesley said. "That's to the east of Lyme Regis, isn't it?"

Katie nodded.

"OK," Lesley said. "You can look into the family in detail in the morning."

She was hurrying down the stairs, the lobby dark apart from the lights on the tree that had been given pride of place right in its centre, when her phone rang.

Sorry, Else. She grabbed it. But it wasn't her wife.

"Jill. How's the investigation going?"

"I hope you don't mind me calling this late."

"You're working on a potentially suspicious death. There's no such thing as late. You've got the name of the widow?" she said.

"Yep. Katie called a few minutes ago. I've got a bit more," Jill told her. "I've had another chat with the witness."

"Tina's mother's friend?"

"Yes, that's the one. Rosamund Winters. So, she's already told us this Roger Gallagher disappeared four years ago. I managed to get more out of her, and a bit from Tina's mum. Apparently, he had a big bust-up with Rosamund's husband, broke off all contact. Rosamund didn't question it. After all, she barely knew him. Maybe they'd just chosen not to remain in touch. But then apparently, her husband started getting cagey about it, so she tried to contact the wife. Sophie."

"Sophie West," Lesley said.

"The thing is, Rosamund initially told me she knew nothing about Roger having any family, then it turns out she knew he had a wife."

"You think that's suspicious?"

"I don't think anything right now. But Rosamund says Sophie wouldn't return her calls. She wouldn't open the door when Rosamund visited. Rosamund says she never saw either of them around Lyme Regis again."

"Maybe they stuck to Charmouth."

"Have you driven through Charmouth?"

Lesley probably had but couldn't remember. "Is it small?"

"That's an understatement. If the Gallaghers weren't going into Lyme, they'd have had to go to Axminster for everything. Or even Exeter."

"That's not far."

"I know. But it's odd."

Odd wasn't enough. "What about the forensics?" Lesley asked. "Has Gail given you anything useful?"

"There's this coat he's wearing," Jill told her. "Or what remains of it. It was orange. It seems that's how Rosamund recognised him. He'd worn it for years, her husband was irritated by it. Said it was too cheap for his golf club."

"The golf club might be worth a visit. If he continued visiting..."

"We looked into it," Jill said. "It closed. The land was bought for flats after a landslip took out two holes."

Lesley was at her car. She opened the driver's door. "Jill," she said.

"Yes, boss?"

"You need to be having this conversation with your team, you know. Not me."

"I know. Sorry."

"Don't apologise. But my role is to oversee, to approve

resource if you need it. To authorise arrest. Your team will help you solve the case." She sat in the driver's seat. "They're a good team, Jill. You need to open up to them."

Silence. Lesley pushed the button to turn her car on. It was bloody freezing in here.

"Jill?"

"Sorry, boss. You're right. I'll talk to the team. First thing."

"Good. But go and see the wife first. She needs to be informed. And find out what she can tell you."

"Katie's looking into the family."

"You can't delay this."

"I know. Sorry, boss. It's been a while since I did this."

Lesley rubbed her hands together. She wanted to be getting home. "You'll be fine, Jill. Have faith in yourself. Let me know in the morning if you need anything from me."

"Will do, boss."

"Oh, and Jill?"

"Yes?"

"Tina Abbott. She's good, and she knows the locals. She'll pick up on things that others might miss. I know she's not in your team, but she's in Lyme Regis at the moment."

"I've spoken to her. It's all a bit incestuous over here, isn't it?"

Lesley chuckled. "It certainly is."

"She's at her mum's. Got a little one with her," Jill said.

"Good. Get her to accompany you when you go and see Sophie, will you?"

"Really?" said Jill. There was a note of surprise in her voice.

"I know she's not on your team," Lesley explained. "And I know we don't normally want people with a personal connection getting involved. But with her local knowledge, she might be able to figure out if Sophie's keeping anything from you."

Silence. Lesley waited.

"Right, boss," Jill said at last. "That makes sense."

CHAPTER THIRTEEN

JILL PULLED up outside Annie Abbott's house. It was low and semi-detached, larger than many of the cottages she'd passed on the way here.

Anning Road was uphill from the old town, with a large playground on a corner and plenty of space for kids to play. She could imagine Tina growing up here, playing on those swings, running down the hill to the beach in the summer. Winter too; she'd heard about their bonkers traditions like the Lyme Lunge.

She got out of the car and looked up and down the road. It was quiet. Just one man out cutting his hedge.

Cutting his hedge in the dark, in December. Either he was a nosy parker, or he was obsessed with tidiness.

She rang the doorbell and waited, blowing on her hands and stamping her feet.

She'd brought her thickest coat. But even that wasn't enough against the bracing seaside air.

The door opened. Mike.

"Hi, Mike," she said. "You're opening your mother-in-law's door."

He shrugged. "Place kinda feels like home."

"That's a good thing. Can you come outside for a moment?"

"No problem, guv." He closed the door behind him, pushing his hands into his armpits. He didn't have a coat on.

"Come and sit in the car with me," she told him. He nodded and hurried to the car, where she let him into the passenger side.

"Is Rosamund at Annie's now?" she asked him.

He cleared his throat. "She is."

Jill nodded, gazing out of the window. The man with the hedge clippers was still there. He kept looking up from his hedge, eyeing them. *A nosy parker, then.*

"Don't get too pally with witnesses," she told him. "It affects your objectivity."

"I'll be fine," he replied. "I've worked cases in Lyme Regis before."

She glanced at him. "If I remember right, you were back at HQ for that case. Tina was on the spot with the DCI."

His jaw clenched. "You're right. I'll be careful."

She eyed him. Trust him, the DCI had said. "I'll just have to trust your judgement."

Truth was, she didn't know Mike, but she had a lot of respect for the DCI. If she trusted him, then Jill would have to.

"The DCI has told me she wants Tina to accompany me to see the victim's wife," she said.

He turned to her, frowning. "Tina? She's not even in our team."

"She's got local knowledge," Jill replied. "The DCI thinks that'll help."

"But I thought you didn't want us getting involved with witnesses."

"This is different. It's about judging whether somebody's telling the truth based on your knowledge of the people and events involved."

He looked ahead, at the road, his hands still in his lap. She wondered if there was professional rivalry between him and Tina.

"Do you mind going in and fetching her?" she asked. "I know she's on leave, but—"

He let out a long breath. "Sure. No problem. Leave means nothing to Tina." He got out of the car.

Jill leaned back, taking in a deep breath.

This was her first major case as head of the Cold Cases Team. She didn't like that it was so close to home.

She picked up her phone while she waited. Meera answered on the second ring.

"Hey, sweetheart," she said. "How's Suzi?"

"Just gone down. I read her *Room on the Broom*."

Jill laughed. "As if you haven't read that to her a hundred times before." She leaned back and listened to Meera telling her what Suzi had done at nursery.

This was what she needed. Familiarity. Family.

CHAPTER FOURTEEN

GAIL HANSFORD SHRUGGED off her forensics kit with a grunt. The salt air whipped at her hair as she stood on the harbour wall, looking out at the grey sea.

What a waste of time.

She'd driven nearly two hours from Swanage for this, leaving Tim with her mum. All for a body so old it was barely more than sea-scraped bones.

Gail didn't like asking the Devon CSI Team to get involved with Dorset cases – she knew it pissed Lesley off – but in this case, it would have made sense.

Ah well. She checked her watch; nearly seven. The drive home would be a dark one, slowed by traffic south of Dorchester. But at least she'd be home in time to give Tim a kiss before he went to sleep. If he was even in bed. About to hit ten years old, he seemed to think he was a grownup.

She hefted her kit and trudged towards her van. The gravel crunched under her feet.

A gull swooped overhead, its cry echoing off the stone buildings.

Gail paused, taking one last look at the harbour. The fishing boats bobbed in the water.

Somewhere out there, a killer was walking free. Or maybe they were miles away by now, or dead themselves.

She shook her head and kept walking; her shoulders slumped.

She reached Holmbush car park at the top of a long, steep hill, her forensics kit heavy in her arms. The rain had started, a fine drizzle that clung to her hair and clothes. If she had to come back here, she'd park further down the hill. But it was unlikely to come to that.

She was fumbling for her keys, eager to get out of the weather and start the long drive home, when movement caught her eye.

A man stood at the edge of the car park, watching her. His face was hidden by the hood of his waterproof jacket.

Gail narrowed her eyes. Something about him seemed off.

She raised her hand in a half-hearted wave, more out of habit than friendliness.

The man turned and walked away; his shoulders hunched against the rain.

Gail frowned. Odd behaviour, but then again, this was an odd town.

She shook her head and unlocked her van. The sooner she got out of here, the better.

As she climbed in, she cast one last glance at where the man had been standing.

Empty now.

Had he ever even been there? Or was she just tired?

CHAPTER FIFTEEN

TINA LEANED FORWARD, elbows on her knees. The living room was warm and cosy, quiet with Mike outside and Louis in bed. Rosamund had just left, finally feeling sufficiently recovered from her shock to go home.

Tension hung in the air.

"You're worried about Rosamund, aren't you?" she asked.

Annie scratched the back of her hand. "The way she reacted when she saw him..."

"I saw how pale she was when she got here."

Annie nodded. "She's not been right for a while."

"How so?"

"I don't know. She gets snappy whenever David's mentioned. I think they've fallen out. And him being a mate of the dead guy..."

"Did you know him? Roger Gallagher?"

Annie tensed. "Never heard his name until today."

Which isn't like you.

"Really? You'd never heard of him?"

Annie shook her head. "I know." She pulled on a smile. "I know everyone, right?"

"Can you remember anything about a man going missing?"

Annie gave her a look. "Tina, love. I'm your mum. You're not on duty here."

"Sorry."

Tina turned at the sound of the front door opening.

Mike poked his head around the living room door. "Sorry to interrupt."

Tina waved him in. "It's fine. Everything OK? Who was at the door?"

He stepped into the room, hands shoved in his pockets. "The boss wants you to visit Roger's wife. Widow."

"I didn't know..." said Annie.

He nodded. "Sophie West. Lives in a big house this side of Charmouth."

Annie perked up. "Now that name I *do* know."

Tina looked at her mum, then at her husband. "But I'm not on the Cold Cases Team."

He shrugged, not meeting her eye. "It's what the boss asked for."

Tina's eyebrows shot up. "The DCI? Or the DI?"

Mike grimaced. "Both, actually."

Tina leaned back. "I see."

"I'm... well, it's not procedure," Mike said. "But I can see their point."

Annie looked between them, confusion on her face.

Tina stood, squeezing her mum's shoulder. "It's fine, Mum. Nothing to worry about."

She turned to Mike. "Maybe it's not a cold case."

He shook his head. "He was last seen four years ago."

"Rosamund wouldn't have been the last person to see him."

His jaw clenched. "Look, we both know what this is about."

She squatted to bring her face level with his; he'd taken one of the ancient armchairs. "Please don't be angry with me, Mike. They just want me cos I'm local."

He looked into her eyes. She knew what he was thinking. He said nothing.

She rubbed the back of his hand. It was cold. He didn't respond.

"When?" she said.

"DI Scott is waiting for you now."

Shit. "OK. Well, Louis is in bed, so—"

"You still haven't eaten," said Annie.

"We can eat when I get back."

"I'll go down to Lyme's."

Fish and Chips. That would fill them all up. "Thanks," Tina said. She squeezed his hand. "I love you."

He blinked, then dragged his gaze up to meet hers. "I love you, too." He put a hand on her stomach. She felt the baby shift.

You know your daddy.

"I'll be as quick as I can."

He shook his head. "You need to be thorough. Her husband's dead."

And that could either mean a grieving widow, or a potential suspect.

"OK," said Tina. "I'll let you know how I get on."

She'd just stood up when a knock sounded at the front door. She hesitated, glancing at her mum.

Her mum shrugged. "I'm not expecting anyone."

Tina went through to the hall and opened the door to find Howard Murchison, her mum's neighbour, standing on the doorstep.

"Hello, Howard." Tina wasn't sure when she'd last known him knock on the door like this.

The elderly man smiled. "Evening, Tina. Just thought I'd pop by and say hello."

Tina frowned. Howard rarely visited, especially unannounced. He'd have seen things happening. He wanted to know the gossip.

Typical Lyme Regis.

"That's... nice of you," she said. "Mum's just in the living room. Would you like to come in?"

Howard shook his head. "Oh no, don't want to intrude. Just wanted to check everything's alright. Noticed a bit of commotion earlier."

"Commotion?"

"Ah, probably nothing," Howard said, waving a hand. "Just thought I'd make sure."

Tina looked past him, to where the DI was waiting in her car. He would be fascinated by that. "Well, thanks for checking. We're all fine here."

Howard gave her a tight smile. "Good, good. I'll be off then. Give my best to your mum."

"Will do. Goodnight, Howard."

Tina waited for him to close the door to his own house, then made for the car. Sometimes, this town drove her mad.

CHAPTER SIXTEEN

LESLEY PUSHED the trolley through IKEA's winding aisles, her mind drifting between sofas and suspects. If she'd remembered this was happening, she'd have stayed in the office longer. Maybe volunteered to go and speak to Sophie West herself.

Southampton IKEA, on a Thursday evening. Not her top choice, especially with the place full of people shopping for Christmas junk. Elsa and Sharon walked ahead, debating the merits of various coffee tables.

"What about this one?" Elsa pointed to a minimalist wooden design.

Lesley shook her head. "Too modern. We need something cosier."

Sharon chuckled. "Never thought I'd hear you say that, Mum."

Elsa looked at Lesley, her expression softening. "You're distracted. Work problems?"

Lesley hesitated. "It's... complex. The body at Lyme Regis. I've brought Tina in."

"Tina?" Elsa's eyebrows raised. "She's in the MCIT. Must be serious."

Lesley shook her head. "She's got local knowledge. But I'm..."

Her family didn't need to know about her concerns. Had she done the right thing, involving Tina? Was it appropriate for her to worry about her team members' marriages?

Focus on your own marriage, she told herself. *Your house move.*

They rounded a corner into the bedroom section. Elsa ran her hand along a metal bedframe. "This could work for the spare room."

Lesley made a noncommittal noise, her thoughts elsewhere.

Elsa nudged her. "Earth to Lesley. What's on your mind?"

Lesley sighed. "Change," Lesley said. "Inter-force politics." She'd been thinking about DI Paterson, who'd be joining them in the new year to head up MCIT.

Dennis, I never thought I'd miss you.

They moved on, to kitchen items. Elsa held up a set of colourful tea towels. "These would brighten up the place."

Lesley forced a smile. "Sure. Chuck them in the trolley."

As they queued for the checkout, Elsa squeezed Lesley's hand. "You'll figure it out. You always do."

Lesley squeezed back, grateful for the support. But she couldn't shake the feeling that this case, and the changes at work, were going to test her. Did she really want to spend her days stuck behind a desk?

Lesley's eyes glazed over as Sharon enthused about the Christmas decorations near the exit. She caught Elsa's gaze and raised an eyebrow.

Elsa nodded, a conspiratorial smile on her lips. "Sharon, love, why don't you pick out what you think works best? Your mum and I are going to grab a coffee."

Sharon wandered off, already engrossed in fairy lights and Swedish-style wooden trinkets.

Lesley felt the tension in her shoulders ease as they made their way to the café. "Thought we'd never escape."

"Admit it," Elsa nudged her. "You only came for the meatballs."

"Guilty as charged." Lesley's lips twitched. She was starving. "Although the company's not bad either."

They settled at a table, tempting plates before them. A third sat steaming on the table; Elsa had messaged Sharon to tell her a plate of meatballs was waiting for her, too. Lesley watched as Elsa stirred her coffee, a familiar warmth spreading through her chest.

"Penny for your thoughts?" Elsa asked.

Lesley hesitated. "Just... thinking about the house."

"Having second thoughts?"

"No." Lesley considered. "It's just... been a while since I've done this."

Elsa reached across the table, squeezing Lesley's hand. "I'm not him, you know."

Lesley nodded, pushing away memories of Terry. They'd moved into the house in Edgbaston when Sharon was five, stretching their budget almost to breaking point. And then she'd gone home after her first week in Dorset to find him there with Julieta. The woman he was now shacked up with in a village outside Solihull, of all places. "I know," she said. "It's different this time."

"It is." Elsa grinned. "I'm much better looking."

Lesley chuckled, the knot in her stomach loosening. "Can't argue with that."

They watched as Sharon approached, pushing a trolley laden with cushions and throws.

"I think I've cracked it," she announced.

"More?" Lesley said. "We already paid."

"Sorry. You don't mind, do you?"

Lesley and Elsa exchanged a fond glance. "No, love," Lesley said. She wanted this to be her daughter's home as much as hers. Sharon was at university in Exeter and barely visited her dad now, despite Lesley's encouragement. Two half-brothers under the age of three didn't help.

Under the table, Lesley felt Elsa's hand slip into hers. She squeezed it, feeling tears come to her eyes. *Don't be mushy*, she told herself.

But she had reason to be mushy. This wasn't like last time. This was right.

—

CHAPTER SEVENTEEN

Tina shifted in the passenger seat as DI Scott drove them towards Charmouth and Sophie's house. The unfamiliar car and unfamiliar colleague left her feeling off-kilter.

"So, what do you know about Sophie?" Jill asked, eyes on the road.

Tina hesitated. "Nothing. Rosamund didn't know anything about her, and my mum recognised the name, but that's all."

The DI nodded. "Right. Any inside info you can give me on her and her husband's relationship?"

Tina sighed. "Lyme's the kind of place where people know each other's business. But they lived in Charmouth. To someone from Lyme, that's a long way away."

The DI smiled. "I know what you mean."

"You live in a small town?"

"Not anymore. We're in Dorchester, But I grew up in the kind of place you're talking about."

Tina couldn't place the DI's accent. But she wasn't about to pry.

"So what do you expect from me here, ma'am? I assume you'll be doing most of the talking."

"Hang on. We're here."

They pulled up outside a large white house. It was generously proportioned, detached with views of the sea. Tina took a deep breath, thinking of the fish and chips Mike was queuing up for right now. Of her son asleep in his dedicated room at Annie's. How would they fit the new baby in, when the time came?

Jill turned to her. "You take the lead. I'll jump in, if needed."

Tina forced herself to close her mouth. Really? She was a DC, and she wasn't even on the investigating team.

But it was an opportunity to prove herself to this new DI. She'd done this before.

"Will do, ma'am."

"And you can call me guv."

"OK. Guv." At least it wasn't *boss*: that would always be the DCI. Had DI Scott worked that out already?

Tina nodded, grateful for the opportunity despite her unease. She stepped out of the car, approaching the house with Jill close behind.

As they reached the door, Tina glanced at her temporary boss. Jill gave her an encouraging nod.

Tina raised her hand and knocked.

Tina's knuckles had barely left the door when it swung open. A woman in her late fifties stood there, her face drawn and pale. She stepped back, wordlessly beckoning them in.

Tina exchanged another glance with the DI and received another nod.

Sophie West, or at least the woman she assumed was Sophie West, led them along a wide hallway with walls covered in family photos to a living room at the Charmouth side of the house. The room stretched from front to back and had windows on three sides, two of those giving views of the sea. Tina could see the lights of Lyme in the distance.

Once they were all in the room, the woman turned to them. "I've been expecting you."

Tina looked back at her. "My name is DC Tina Abbott. This is DI Jill Scott."

"I know why you're here. It's about Roger."

Tina frowned. If Sophie had reported Roger missing, that would have been years ago. So...

"You know?" she prompted.

A nod. "People talk around here. I heard from Claire who works in the bookshop, who heard from Eddie at the harbour."

She didn't seem to be grieving.

"Ms West," Tina said. "Would you like to take a seat?" She gestured towards the grey leather sofa. "I think—"

"I know you found Roger's body in the harbour. And I know he's been in the water for years." She was still standing.

Tina felt a prickle of unease. Sophie's calm seemed forced, rehearsed even. She glanced at the DI, who was gazing out towards the sea. Was there access to a secluded spot where a man could throw himself in, from here? Or maybe get himself pushed?

"Ms West," Tina said, "we need to know who you've spoken to about your husband's death."

Sophie's eyes narrowed. "Why? He committed suicide."

"You know that?"

"He wasn't a happy man. A lot of people pissed him off, and he pissed them off in turn." The woman folded her arms across her chest. "Including me."

Tina turned at the sound of a door slamming. Footsteps sounded in the adjacent hallway and a tall man with fair hair entered. He had an air of propriety, as if he was more than comfortable in this house.

"Soph?" he said. "Everything alright?"

Sophie West softened. The man stepped towards her, all but pushing the DI out of the way. He pulled her into an embrace. She didn't take her eyes off Tina.

"This is Mark," she said. "My husband. After two years of hearing nothing from Roger, I was granted a divorce."

Tina nodded. So Sophie West was no grieving widow. She looked at the man. "Could I take your full name please?"

"Mark Coombs. What's this about?"

"Your wife's former husband—"

"Roger? What's that bastard been up to now?" Mark tightened his grip on his wife.

"It's alright, Mark," Sophie said. "Roger's dead. Definitely dead."

He looked down at her, eyes widening. "How?"

"Mr Coombs," said the DI. Tina was relieved to have her step in. "Ms West. Roger's body was pulled out of Lyme Regis harbour early this morning. We have reason to believe he went into the water at least three y—"

"Drowned, eh?" said the man. "So the coward killed himself, then."

"We don't know that."

"Can we all sit down?" Tina suggested. "We do need to ask you some questions."

Mark eyed her. "You think we killed him."

"Right now, we don't know how he died. There's no reason to suspect that—"

"But you know how much we hated him. He hurt my wife, you know?"

"Mark," Sophie said, her tone firm.

"Sorry, love, but it's true. The world's a better place without him."

"Don't. There's the children."

Tina looked at the DI. There'd been no mention of children.

She needed to take control of this conversation. "Ms West, Mr Coombs. Why don't we all sit down? Maybe I can make a cup of tea..."

"Are you one of those liaison officers?" Mark asked.

"No. I'm just—"

"Let's just all sit down and have a quick chat," DI Scott said. "The sooner you answer our questions, the sooner we'll be out of your hair."

"Of course," Sophie said. Tina looked at the woman's husband. It seemed she had a taste for domineering men, if what he'd said was to be believed.

"Tell us about Roger," the DI said, her voice calm but firm.

Sophie's shoulders tensed. "What do you want to know?"

"Your relationship. His disappearance. Start from the beginning."

Sophie sighed. "We argued. He said he wanted to leave me. Then he left."

Tina frowned. That wasn't exactly *the beginning*. And something in Sophie's tone didn't ring true.

"How long were you together?" Jill asked.

Sophie's laugh was bitter. "Sixteen years. Long enough to have two children. Not that he gave a fuck about them."

"Roger wasn't a good man, officers," said Mark. "He was

abusive. Cruel. Leaving Sophie was the best thing he ever did for her."

Sophie shook her head. "He... he wasn't violent."

"Coercive control," her husband muttered. "It's still abuse, love."

Sophie blinked. She looked cowed. *Out of the frying pan, into the fire*, Tina thought.

Sophie nodded, her eyes filling with tears. "Emotionally. Financially. He controlled everything."

"Did you ever consider speaking to anyone?" Tina asked.

Sophie's gaze met hers. "The police? Would you have believed me?"

Sophie's mobile rang, breaking the tension. Sophie glanced at the screen, her shoulders visibly relaxing.

"It's Mhairi," she said, a hint of relief in her voice. "My daughter. Do you mind if I...?"

Tina nodded. "Of course."

Sophie left the room, Mark following her.

"What do you think?" the DI muttered.

Tina shook her head. "She isn't grieving. But we don't even know how he died yet."

The guv nodded. "Still, I think we need to keep an eye on both of them. Can you find out if she was seeing Mark before Roger disappeared?"

"My mum might be able to get that on the grapevine. If you're sure..."

The DI nodded. "That's not a question I expect this pair to answer honestly. But be discreet."

"I will."

Sophie entered, wiping her cheeks. "Sorry."

The DI stood up. "That's fine. Is your daughter local?"

"Southampton."

"And will she be coming home?"

Sophie looked puzzled. "Home?"

"To support you? We can find out a liaison officer, to help out. I'll put that in train."

Sophie's eyes widened. "Oh. She... she might be. I'm not sure."

Tina frowned. Had she even told her daughter about Roger's death?

Jill leaned forward. "Ms West, would you like us to inform your daughter about her father's death?"

A sniff. "Yes. Yes please."

Wow. So she hadn't even told her.

Why?

One thing was for sure. However well her mum did or didn't know Sophie, Tina would need to get as much gossip on this woman as she could.

CHAPTER EIGHTEEN

MIKE SHIFTED on Annie's floral sofa. The constant stream of women in and out of the house was making him uneasy. And now she was watching more of them on TV: *Call the Midwife*. He glanced at his watch, wondering how long Tina would be.

The doorbell rang. Annie hurried to answer it.

"Rosamund, love. And Cameron, too. Come in, come in."

Mike straightened as Rosamund entered, her son trailing behind. He'd met the lad before, although he was more of a young man now. Had he grown that much, in a year?

And why was Rosamund back?

"Cameron has something to tell you," Rosamund said, her voice tight.

Annie gestured for them to sit. "What is it, Cam?"

Cameron remained silent, his shoulders hunched.

"Go on," Rosamund urged. "Tell them what you told me."

The young man's voice was low. "It's about Mhairi."

Mike leaned forward. "Mhairi?"

"Sophie's daughter," said Rosamund. "Roger's daughter."

Ah. Why hadn't they uncovered a daughter?

Cameron swallowed. "She told me... her dad used to hurt her."

The room fell silent.

"When was this?" Mike asked, keeping his tone gentle.

"Ages ago. Before she left." Cameron's gaze moved around the room. "She said he'd hurt her when she was cheeky."

Cheeky? Mike's jaw clenched. "Did she say *how* he hurt her?"

Cameron shook his head. "Just that it was bad. That's why she never comes home."

"But her dad's gone now," Annie whispered.

Cameron looked up, his eyes hard. "She said her mum should've protected her. But she didn't."

Annie put a hand on Rosamund's shoulder. Rosamund was pale still, her face impassive.

Mike stood up. He needed to remind them all of why he was here. It wasn't Annie who was SIO, although it wasn't him, either.

"Thank you, Cameron," he said. "We appreciate you providing this information. Where is Mhairi living now?"

"Southampton. She went to uni, never came back. Her mum won't know where she is. No one here does."

"Can we get home now?" Rosamund asked. "Cameron's tired."

And so are you, Mike thought, looking at the dark circles under her eyes. He nodded. "Thanks." He looked at Cameron. "Do you have any way of contacting her?"

A shrug. "I might be able to find her in a Discord server. I'll check."

"I'd appreciate that."

Rosamund raised her eyebrows at him, and he nodded. Annie ushered them out, then returned.

"You look done in," she said. "Would you like a biscuit?"

"No, thanks." The fish and chips had been more than filling. He'd tried to wait for Tina to return, but his rumbling stomach had got the better of him. Hers was in the oven, under a low heat.

"I need some air," he said.

He slipped out the front door, grateful for the crisp evening breeze. Across the street, the neighbour Howard was perched precariously on a stepladder, wrestling with a tangle of Christmas lights.

Mike pulled out his phone. His first instinct was to call Tina, but she would be busy. The DI, too. He scrolled to Stanley's number instead.

He answered on the third ring. "Mike? I'm just leaving the station."

"Stan, do you know anything about a Mhairi? Roger's daughter."

"We've been focused on the wife. A daughter? How old?"

"Early twenties, I guess. I've just been speaking to her friend Cameron. He's the son of the woman who recognised Roger."

Stanley laughed. "Blimey Mike, you do get 'em."

He pushed back irritation. "This is important."

"Sorry, mate. What about the daughter?"

"Her dad hurt her, apparently. Physical abuse. She hasn't been home in years. But we need to find her. She could be a suspect."

CHAPTER NINETEEN

LESLEY GRIPPED the steering wheel as she navigated the busy Southampton streets. It was eight am and the rush hour was in full flow. The satnav blinked, guiding them towards the outskirts of town.

Katie fidgeted in the passenger seat.

"Will you stop that?" Lesley snapped.

"Sorry." Katie clenched her fists in her lap. Lesley wasn't sure if that was more annoying.

"OK," she said. "Remind me what you've got on Mhairi Gallagher."

"Twenty-two years old, graduated from Southampton this summer just gone. She's going by Mhairi Jones now."

"So it must have been bad, what he did to her."

Katie wrinkled her nose. "Poor woman."

"She might be a murderer."

"But we don't even know he was murdered."

Lesley sniffed. She wasn't supposed to be out interviewing witnesses. Carpenter would be pissed off. But it was easier to beg forgiveness than ask for permission, and her DI was two hours away. More.

Lesley sighed. "OK. Let me talk to her, you just look young and sympathetic. It might make her more likely to open up."

"Will we be asking her about the abuse?"

Lesley slowed at a set of traffic lights. These roads were unfamiliar, but at least she wasn't on a narrow country lane.

"Let's see what she tells us, eh? The most important thing is to establish if she knows her father's dead. Her mother didn't tell her, apparently."

Katie nodded. "I reckon we shouldn't tell her, either, then. Let her—"

Lesley glanced sideways with an amused smile. "You reckon, do you?"

Katie bit her lip. "Sorry, boss."

Lesley sniggered, and it occurred to her that if she allowed herself to be amused by Katie, the DC didn't annoy her so much. And she seemed to quite like causing amusement.

Takes all sorts.

They turned onto a quiet residential street. Rows of identical flats lined both sides.

"This is it," Lesley said, pulling up to the kerb. She cut the engine and turned to Katie. "Ready?"

Katie nodded, her face serious. "Flat 2b, boss. Of course."

They climbed out of the car and approached Mhairi's flat. Lesley took a deep breath. The air here felt thicker than in Bournemouth.

The flat was on the second floor of a three-storey block with an exposed staircase and walkways. Litter lined the staircase, and the place had a familiar smell of decay. Lesley rapped on the door. After a moment it swung open, revealing a sullen-faced young woman.

"Mhairi Jones?" Lesley asked.

The woman took a step back, her face tight. "Who wants to know?"

Lesley gave her a smile. "You don't need to worry, Mhairi. Sorry if we gave you a shock. I'm DCI Clarke, this is DC Young. We'd like to ask you some questions about your father."

Mhairi's jaw tightened. She looked past them, then stepped back another pace. "Come in, then."

They followed her into a sparsely furnished living room. Lesley perched on the edge of an armchair while Katie hovered nearby.

"When did you last see your father?" Lesley asked.

Mhairi shrugged. "Dunno. Years ago."

"Can you be more specific?"

"No."

Lesley felt Katie shift beside her, itching to interject. She shot her a warning glance.

"Am I right in thinking you left home after your A Levels, and you haven't been back since?"

"Maybe."

Lesley smiled. "You're not in any trouble, Mhairi." *Not yet, at least.* "We've received reports that your father—"

"He's dead, isn't he?"

"How do you know that?"

A shrug. "I've got mates. People I keep in touch with." She looked between Lesley and Katie. "No one who's still in Charmouth or Lyme, I'm not that stupid. But word spreads. And I saw it online, the body dragged out of the harbour. I'd know that orange coat anywhere."

The orange coat. That was how Rosamund had recognised him, too. Lesley gave Katie a look and the DC wrote something in her notepad.

"How do you feel about your father's death?" Lesley asked.

Mhairi laughed. "I didn't kill him, if that's what you're thinking. How long's he been in there? Probably killed himself after he realised what kind of man he was."

She was right; they still didn't know if Roger's death was murder. She hoped Stanley was making some progress with Pathology. God, she hated it when bodies had to be taken over to Devon.

"Do you travel to Charmouth or Lyme Regis at all, Mhairi? Visit your mum?"

"No. Never. She can come here if she wants, but I'm not going back there."

Lesley nodded. "And does she? Come here?"

Mhairi wiped an eye. "No."

"Mhairi, when was the last time you were in Lyme Regis?"

Mhairi glared back at her. Lesley waited. She resisted the urge to look at Katie: *keep quiet*.

Eventually, Mhairi sniffed. "Four years, I reckon. Four years and... three months. I came here for uni, did a four-year course. Now I'm working at the Ordnance Survey offices. Not causing anyone any trouble." She licked her lips. "So I'd be grateful if you could leave me alone. Stop raking up things I'd rather forget."

CHAPTER TWENTY

JILL YAWNED as she steered her car along the winding coastal road. The sky was lightening, streaks of pink and orange painting the horizon. She'd left Dorchester well before dawn, eager to get an early start in Lyme Regis.

As she rounded a bend, the sea came into view. The morning sun glinted off the water, turning it to molten gold. Despite her fatigue, Jill couldn't help but admire the beauty.

She passed the turnoff to West Bay with no traffic to bother her. It wasn't long before Charmouth, the Gallagher house, and then the turnoff to Lyme.

Her phone rang. She answered on the hands-free.

"DI Scott."

"Morning, detective inspector." It was Dr Bamford, the pathologist. "I've got some information on your victim."

Jill's grip tightened on the steering wheel. "Go on."

"Well first off, we have a cause of death. It wasn't drowning."

"What was it?"

"Asphyxiation. Even with a body this old, immersion in

water slows decomposition, so we were able to identify lesions in his throat consistent with strangulation. And there was water in his lungs, but not the kind of damage we'd expect from drowning. I think it's fair to say he wasn't in water when he died."

"So he was murdered."

"Not for me to judge, detective."

She rolled her eyes. *Pathologists.* She'd put up with Henry Whittaker for years and hoped this guy would be better.

"We found remnants of fabric adhering to his skin and inside his windpipe. What seems to be blue denim and some pale cotton, which might have been any colour originally. And there's the boot still on his foot, although badly decomposed."

"What about the orange coat?" She'd wondered what it was made of, for a large chunk of it to have survived this long still wrapped around his torso.

"It's Gore-tex, hence the resistance to water damage. I can send you photos so you can work on identifying a brand."

"Nothing as handy as a label?"

She heard a snigger. *So you are human.* "No. Sorry."

"Anything else?"

"We found something interesting in his inside pocket. A commemorative coin."

Jill frowned. "What kind of coin?"

"It's from a music festival. Dated three and a half years ago. Summer 2021."

Jill's mind raced. "So he was alive then."

"It appears so."

"Thanks, doctor. Send those photos to the team inbox, please."

Jill ended the call, her earlier tranquillity forgotten. She pressed down on the accelerator as she turned towards Lyme Regis.

Her phone rang again. She answered, keeping her eyes on the winding road.

"DI Scott."

"It's DCI Clarke. We've just finished interviewing Mhairi."

Jill felt her pulse pick up. "How did it go?"

"She's a traumatised young woman. Hasn't gone back to Lyme since her A Levels four years ago."

"But Sophie said she visited... Once or twice a year. That's what I think she said."

"Perhaps Sophie was trying to cover something up."

The road dropped in front of Jill and a view of the town opened up. It was beautiful, she had to admit. "What's your take on her?"

"She doesn't seem like a killer to me. Anyway, I'll leave it with you."

"Boss?"

"Yes?"

"I've just been speaking to Dr Bamford. He says the victim died of asphyxiation."

"Not drowning?"

"Not drowning."

"Not related to being in water? Strangulation by his clothes?"

"He didn't seem to think so." Should she have pressed him? "No. He said the pattern of water in his lungs was inconsistent. He wasn't in water when he died."

"OK, then."

Jill waited. The DCI said nothing.

"OK then?" she prompted.

"What's your next move, DI Scott?"

Jill pulled in a breath, reminding herself to slow down as the lanes narrowed. What was her next move?

There was the family feud, if that was what it was. The fact that Roger had certainly abused Mhairi, and possibly Sophie, too.

"I need to speak to Pathology again," she said. "And Forensics. We need to establish how much strength would have been needed to kill him this way. And see if we can trace his movements four years ago."

"Four years?"

"Pathology found a coin in the pocket of his clothes. Dates back four years."

"You want to work out exactly when he died? See if we can determine his movements?"

"I do, boss."

"Well, then you do that. A case like this isn't going to be solved with forensics alone. Probably not CCTV or any of the evidence we're used to working with."

"I know." This was why Jill had applied for the job.

"Good. Find out what else you can from people who might have known him. You're doing well, Jill. Keep it up."

Jill pumped a fist on the steering wheel.

Good.

Her first murder case, and her new DCI was showing trust in her.

CHAPTER TWENTY-ONE

KATIE STIFLED a yawn as she entered the office. Saturday mornings had never been her favourite, especially when Christmas was so close. She'd done most of her shopping weeks ago, but there were always the last-minute gifts, especially for her mum. She probably wouldn't appreciate whatever Katie bought her, but she'd be getting something nice anyway.

She slumped into her chair, the squeak of its wheels echoing in the near-empty room. A few desks over, someone from the IT Team tapped away at a keyboard. The hum of the air conditioning provided a low background drone.

Katie reached for her phone, scrolling mindlessly through social media. *Just five more minutes*, she told herself.

"Morning, Katie. Fancy a coffee?"

She looked up to see Stanley hovering by the door. *You're early.*

"No, I'm fine," Katie mumbled, putting down her phone.

Stanley lingered for a moment before shuffling away. Katie winced, realising how abrupt she'd been.

"Actually, Stanley?" she called after him. "A coffee would be great, thanks."

He turned to give her a small smile and headed for the break room.

Sighing, Katie turned to her computer and logged in. She'd been working on a search of Roger Gallagher's history and trying to access the divorce papers from when Sophie had finally given him up for dead.

There was an email from the court: divorce papers and accompanying correspondence.

Sophie West had applied for a divorce two years to the day from when she had last seen her husband. She'd had to prove that he'd been uncontactable, and that none of his associates or friends had seen him. She'd certainly been made to jump through the hoops.

And as his ex-wife rather than his widow, she'd had to agree to a financial settlement with the courts that didn't involve her appropriating all his property as she would have done if he had died while they were still married.

The house was still jointly owned, and there was his business. She'd become a fifty per cent shareholder.

And then there was the cash.

The documents showed £550,000 in personal accounts held in Roger's name. His company bank account contained only £232.

Katie frowned.

She leaned back, staring at the figures. Roger was person-ally wealthy. Sophie had been required to submit informa-tion on her own bank accounts, too. There had been £12,000 in her savings account, a little under £2,000 in her current account and just £32 in a joint current account.

£550,000. Had Sophie known about that money before

her husband disappeared? Had he earned it through his company? If he had, why hadn't he left it there? The business looked like it was broke.

Had Sophie been accessing that money before applying for the divorce? Or was something else going on here?

She jumped as Stanley put a mug on her desk.

"Sorry," he said. "You look miles away."

She pointed at her screen. "Roger Gallagher's finances. They're off."

He wrinkled his nose, bending over to lean into the screen. Reading the figures, he whistled. "Someone could have killed him for the cash."

"If they did, they didn't get it."

Not even Sophie. Not for two years, anyway.

She put a hand on the mug and looked up at Stanley. "We need to speak to Companies House. Find out if he got that money through the business."

Stanley nodded. "Or some other way."

CHAPTER TWENTY-TWO

Jɪʟʟ ᴀᴘᴘʀᴏᴀᴄʜᴇᴅ ᴛʜᴇ ᴛᴀᴋᴇᴀᴡᴀʏ ᴋɪᴏsᴋ, squinting against the bright sunlight that reflected off the sea. The small wooden structure stood between Monmouth Beach and the Cobb, the air around it thick with the smell of fried food and salt.

A young man who had to be Cameron Winters was inside, wiping down the counter. He looked up as Jill neared, his face tightening with recognition.

"DI Scott," he said, his tone wary. "What can I do for you?"

Jill leaned against the counter. *So you know who I am.* "I need to ask you some questions about Mhairi."

Cameron's shoulders tensed. He looked around, as if trying to identify an escape route.

"What about her?"

"You were friends. You've already told us that she left home because her father was abusive. Did she ever talk to you about her parents' relationship?"

He hesitated, conflict clear on his face. "Look, I don't want to betray her confidence."

"Cameron, we've found her dad's body. This is serious."

Cameron ran a hand through his hair. It was mid-brown, floppy. Full of some kind of product. "OK. She didn't say much, but... I got the impression things weren't great between them."

"How so?"

He shrugged. "Well, I never saw the two of them together, for one. In fact, I never saw her dad in Lyme. Her mum used to come in all the time. She hasn't much recently." He let out a short laugh. "Not that she'd stoop to getting her food here."

"They're wealthy."

"There are plenty of people around here who're loaded. It's not exactly a cheap place to live. And my mum... Well, she does alright. But yeah. Mhairi's parents were a cut above. Acted that way, too."

Jill frowned. "When was the last time you spoke to her?"

Cameron shrugged. "Couple of months ago, maybe? We don't talk much these days."

"Does she come back to Lyme Regis at all? Family visits, that kind of thing?" It was Christmas, after all.

He shook his head. "No. I've seen her two or three times since she went to uni. Two times I went to Southampton, another we met in Bournemouth. She never comes back here."

"And you haven't seen her recently."

"No. Sorry."

So it looked like Mhairi had been telling the truth to the DCI. She gave him a smile. "Can I get some chips?"

"It's breakfast time. We're not doing them yet, sorry."

"OK. A sausage butty or something?"

"Yeah. Give me a minute."

She turned away from the kiosk while he busied himself, watching the seagulls swooping over the harbour. A woman was bending over a small child, flapping her arms.

She smiled. *Guess I'd better be careful with my butty.*

Movement caught her eye, and she shifted to see a man standing next to the RNLI building, watching her. He wore a dark blue coat and a black beanie and was shuffling his feet, his gaze intent on her.

She met his gaze for a few moments, until he turned away and began to walk towards the Cobb.

"Who's that?" she asked, turning to Cameron and pointing.

Tom squinted against the sun. "Oh, him? I think he's one of Annie's neighbours. Covers his house in lights every year."

Jill watched the man as he walked away, occasionally glancing over his shoulder towards her. He was elderly, with a paunch that spoke of too many pints at the local.

"Has he been there long?"

Tom shrugged. "Didn't notice him before. You've caused a bit of a stir; people will want to know what you're up to."

She sighed. *Small towns.* He was right.

"Here you are."

He placed the sandwich on the counter. It looked good.

She turned to see that the man had stopped at the point where the Cobb forked left. He was watching her still. *Maybe he's got information.*

"Thanks, Cameron." She grabbed her sandwich and strolled towards the Cobb, her steps measured. As she neared the man, he looked back at her. His eyes widened and he took a step away.

"Afternoon," she called out. "Can I help you with something?"

The man stopped, not turning to face her. "Just... curious, is all."

Jill had carried on walking, and now she was just a few feet away from him.

"About?" she asked.

He gestured towards the kiosk. "Saw you talking to young Cameron. Wondered if it was about Roger."

Jill's eyes narrowed. "Is there anything you'd like to talk to us about? We're keen to speak to anyone who might have information."

The man looked away again, suddenly finding the horizon fascinating. "No, nothing in particular. Just... interested, you know? Concerned."

Jill didn't believe him for a second. "What's your name, sir?"

He sighed, shoulders slumping. "Howard Murchison."

"OK, Mr Murchison, well if you do think of anything that might be useful to us, here's my number." She held out her card and he took it, stuffing it into a pocket without looking at it.

"Right," he said.

Jill stepped back towards the town, pulling out her phone. She dialled Meera's number. It was Saturday, and her wife would actually be able to enjoy the day off they'd both hoped to share.

"Hey, love. It's me."

"How's Lyme Regis?"

Jill sighed. "This place is something else. So many relationships. So many busybodies."

Meera laughed. "That's not just Lyme Regis, you know. It's half of Dorset."

Jill leaned against a nearby wall. "And I'm getting nowhere with this case. His wife and daughter both had motives, but neither of them big enough for me to imagine them strangling him then manhandling him into the sea."

"He lived on the clifftop, didn't he?"

"Yes."

"Maybe they pushed him off."

"The position of the house is all wrong. The slope isn't steep enough."

"OK. Any other suspects?"

"Not yet." Her phone buzzed: Katie. She pushed back a sigh. "I've got to go."

"Course. You should be having this conversation with Mike, you know."

Jill closed her eyes. She could feel a headache coming on. She tore open the wrapper off the sausage butty. *I need this.* "You're right. I know you're right."

"Where is Mike, anyway?" Meera asked.

Jill frowned, realising she hadn't seen him yet this morning. "I don't know, actually. He should be here."

"Maybe he's at his mum's?"

"Mother-in-law's. Anyway, sorry. I've got to take another call."

"You've got this, my love. It'll be fine."

"Yeah. Give Suzi a kiss from me."

"Will do." Meera hung up.

Jill switched to the call from Katie, hoping the DC had something useful for her.

CHAPTER TWENTY-THREE

MIKE SAT at Annie's kitchen table, cradling a mug of tea. Tina had taken Louis out for a walk and, he suspected, to buy him a Christmas present. He'd overheard her moaning to her mum about the scarf he'd requested. The house was quiet, the only sound the occasional seagull outside.

Annie bustled about, wiping down counters. "It's nice to have a moment of peace, isn't it? Though I do love your little one's giggles."

Mike nodded, unable to resist a smile. "He can be a handful."

Annie's gaze softened as she turned to him. "You're doing a wonderful job with him, you know. Both of you are. And he's going to love having a little brother or sister."

"Thanks," Mike said, shifting in his seat. He was worried about how they would cope with four of them in their tiny two-bedroomed house. While the baby was in their room it would be fine, but then what? They wouldn't be able to afford a move unless one of them made sergeant.

And he had a feeling that wasn't going to be him.

He cleared his throat. "Annie, I wanted to ask you about Roger's disappearance. Do you remember anything about him disappearing? I know it was Rosamund who knew him, but—"

"She didn't really know him, love. David, that's her husband. He's the one who knew him."

He nodded. They'd tried to get hold of David, but Rosamund said he was on a business trip abroad. And he'd stopped seeing Roger before the other man had disappeared, so it seemed unlikely he'd be able to help them.

Unless...

"You haven't asked me if I knew Sophie," Annie said.

Mike looked up. Annie was leaning against the kitchen sink, wiping her hands on a tea towel.

"Sorry?" he said. "You know her?"

"No more than I know anyone around here. But yes, we were on nodding terms. Until a couple of years ago, when she stopped coming into Lyme. I just assumed she'd moved away."

"Why did you think that?"

A shrug. "She was depressed. Or miserable, anyway. Same thing, isn't it?"

He stared at his mother-in-law. If she knew Sophie, why hadn't she said anything?

Don't get annoyed. She was more than just a witness. She was the grandmother of his child. Children, soon.

He took a breath. "How do you know she was depressed?"

A shrug. "She was a friendly enough woman most of the time. I barely knew her— – knew her name, of course, I know lots of people's names – but didn't know her well enough to go for a drink with her or anything. But we chatted from time to time, in the queue at the butcher's. Waiting for a bus. That kind of thing."

"And what did she say? When was this?"

Annie shook her head. "I can't really remember, son. But it was probably three or four years ago. Last time I saw her was when they switched the Christmas tree lights on in..." She closed her eyes. "November. Four years ago. Yes, that's right, 'cause Tina was here and you weren't. Last time she did something like that without you."

Mike felt his cheeks redden. "And she was depressed then?"

A nod.

He pushed back the urge to grit his teeth. "Annie, I need you to be more specific. What was she doing that made you think that?"

"Crying. She wept while they turned the lights on. Poor woman. I was up on the raised bit, you know, by the bookshop. She was down on the road. So I couldn't speak to her. But I saw her."

Mike nodded. "And that was the last time you saw her."

Annie screwed up her face, then nodded. "Although there were the rumours."

He leaned forward. "What rumours?"

"Well, according to Grant in the chippy, she paid off her mortgage."

How would someone in the chippy know that? But Mike knew better than to ask.

"She paid off her mortgage."

A nod. "All of a sudden, Mike. Three years ago, that was, and I never heard anything about her again. Didn't know her Roger was friends with Rosamund's David. Didn't even know she was still living up at that house." She shuddered. "Poor woman."

"OK. Anything else you remember?"

Annie gave him a smile, her face suddenly open and bright again. "Nothing, sorry love. D'you want another cuppa?"

He heard the sound of the door opening and Tina's voice. He felt his body slump. The conversation would turn to Christmas plans and pregnancy. Annie's brief moment of opening up to him was gone.

But was it relevant? Sophie's depression, or unhappiness, at least, and the fact that she'd supposedly paid off her mortgage?

Was it relevant to her husband's death, or just more local gossip?

CHAPTER TWENTY-FOUR

JILL LEANED AGAINST THE DESK, her eyes fixed on the phone in the centre of the table. The muffled cries of seagulls and the distant sound of the sea drifted through the open window.

"Right, let's get everyone up to speed," she said. "Mike and I are in Lyme Regis." They were in the police station in Hill Road. Mike had called saying he had some new information, and she'd asked him to join her there. "Boss, can you hear us?"

"We're here," the DCI's voice crackled through the speaker.

Mike sat down in one of the plastic chairs and looked up at her, then hesitated. She smiled and sat next to him, leaning over the table.

"OK, so here's where we're at. It seems that Roger went missing three and a half years ago, according to the PM."

"The commemorative coin that was found in his pocket," the DCI said.

"Yes, that. He doesn't seem to have been a popular man;

the only person who was friendly with him is David Winters. That's the husband of Rosamund, the woman who recognised Roger from the remnants of his orange coat."

"What about the post-mortem?" the DCI asked.

Jill nodded. "He didn't drown. He was strangled. Someone killed him, then pushed him into the sea to make it look like an accident. I don't imagine they expected it would take three years for his body to wash back up."

She swallowed, trying not to imagine Roger's body drifting in the currents for all that time. He didn't sound like the most pleasant of men, but...

"His family have motive," she continued. "His wife was clearly unhappy in their relationship, and it sounds like he was abusive. And he was certainly abusive to their daughter, but there's no evidence of her having even been in Lyme Regis for over four years."

"Surely she could have travelled here without anyone knowing," said Katie over the phone.

"She could," Jill agreed. "But no one seems to have seen her. And to do that by public transport..."

"It's quite a journey," said Mike. "Two trains and a local bus that hardly ever runs."

She nodded.

"One of her mates could have given her a lift," Stanley pointed out. "Cameron Winters, maybe."

Jill chewed the end of her pen. Meera had bought her a nice Parker pen for her last birthday, but it languished at the bottom of her bag, neglected in favour of cheaper alternatives she could chew on without guilt. "He could. I spoke to him, and he didn't seem suspicious. But we can't rule it out."

"And I assume there are no useful forensics," said the DCI.

"Apart from that coin, no."

"I've got something," Katie said. Jill heard muttering at the other end of the line, then Katie's voice came back, clearer this time.

"So I've been looking at records of the divorce. After he went missing, because there wasn't a body, his wife couldn't have him pronounced dead. But after two years, she could get a divorce. She had to provide evidence that he was uncontactable. And in order to access a portion of his finances, she had to provide financial evidence, both with regard to herself and to him."

"She must be loaded," Mike said. "That's a big house, sea views—"

"Well, it's off," said Katie. "Roger's financial situation. There was no cash in his company, no sign of much in the way of money owing to the business, either. I've looked through Companies House records and it looks like he was in the process of winding it down."

"Maybe going bust?" Jill suggested. "What was it he did?"

"Logistics. But that's not what was odd. Roger himself had savings totalling over half a million pounds."

Mike whistled. "Well, that would be a motive."

"How much of this was Sophie able to access?" Jill asked.

"Half of it, once she'd waited the two years and got the divorce," Katie said. "She'll get the rest, now he's officially dead."

Jill nodded.

"That fits," Mike said.

Jill turned to him. "Fits?"

"With what Annie just said to me. That's what I wanted to talk to you about. She said Sophie was depressed, four years ago. That doesn't really make sense, unless..." He shook his head. "The important thing is, she paid off her mortgage. According to the local rumours."

"She did," Katie said. "I've got the deeds right here. The house transferred from Santander to Sophie West in its entirety eighteen months ago.

Mike frowned. "That's not what Annie heard."

"I thought you said she paid off her mortgage?" Annie said.

He nodded. "But she heard the rumour three years ago..." He shook his head. "She just got it wrong, I imagine."

Jill turned back to the phone. "So is there anything else."

"There is," said the boss. "Stanley?"

"Yeah." Jill hadn't heard Stanley speak more than three or four times since she'd started in the job. She needed to make more of an effort to get to know him. "He was a local councillor. On the planning committee."

"That fits," Jill said. She knew the type; playing golf with local businessmen, networking with the people they thought were important.

"He lost his seat after one term," Stanley said. "Seems he was unpopular. I've found some reports in the local papers about unpopular planning applications being green-lit."

Jill frowned. "So, we have a potential motive there? As well as the abuse within the family?"

"You can't rule anything out at this point," said the boss. Jill sighed. She'd been so looking forward to not spending Christmas driving back and forth across the county.

"Hang on," Katie said. "I'm on the planning website now. I can see some... some questionable approvals. Applications I can't imagine ever getting passed." She cleared her throat. "My dad's a builder, I know a bit about this stuff."

Mike leaned forward. "What's our next move?"

Jill straightened up. "We keep digging. Stanley, I want you to focus on Roger's financials. Get bank account statements for the period leading up to his death, and the period when he was on the planning committee. Katie, continue looking into the planning applications. Find out which were the most contentious. Mike, you speak to the people affected. We might have another suspect out there."

"You can't forget the widow and daughter," the boss said.

Jill sighed. "You spoke to Mhairi. What was your take on her?"

"She seemed to genuinely not know her father was dead. And... well, she didn't act suspiciously. But she's had three years to perfect her story, if it is her."

"Yes. OK, we'll talk to Sophie again. Meanwhile, let's see what we can get on those planning applications, and the cash. We need to know who else Roger Gallagher pissed off, and if that's why he died."

CHAPTER TWENTY-FIVE

SOPHIE WEST'S house was impressive. Very different from the low cottages that tumbled towards the harbour in the centre of Lyme Regis

The view out to sea was breathtaking, and the position at the top of the cliffs made Mike pause for thought. But they'd already checked, and they knew it would be impossible to push someone off from here. Too many overhangs, ledges and undulations below.

He followed the guv up the wide gravel driveway and waited as she rang the doorbell.

No answer.

She looked past him, around the driveway. A blue Ford SUV was parked there. In the same spot as the DI had told him it had been last night. Sophie's car, he presumed. There wasn't much you could walk to from here, but there was the coastal path. Maybe she'd gone out for some exercise.

The DI pushed on the buzzer again. She leaned forward and pushed the letterbox open, then let it fall.

"Shit."

He frowned. "What's up?"

"There's a man in there."

There's a new bloke, isn't there?"

"It's not him. He's older." She frowned. "Does Sophie have a father locally?"

He shrugged. "Not that I know of. You want me to check?"

She shook her head. "It doesn't look like she's in, Mike. Let's come back later."

Her voice was loud, almost shouting. What was going on?

She grabbed him by the arm and yanked him away from the door to a spot in front of the garage where they couldn't be seen from inside.

"What's happening?" he asked.

She put a finger to her lips. "Shush."

He waited. Would she explain herself? Or was she one of those bosses who just told you what to do without explanation, and didn't think you needed to know? He'd had a couple of those in Uniform.

"The man in the house," she whispered. "I think I've seen him, watching us. Apart from Sophie's, there's no car here." She cast around with her hand. "So where did he come from? And if he's in there and Sophie isn't...?"

He nodded. "What d'you want us to do, guv?"

"I want to go around the back of the house and get a better view of him. See if there's a way in."

"You want to arrest him?"

She frowned. "We don't have any reason to arrest him, Mike."

"I didn't... I just..."

"I know. Sorry, I'm being weird. But there's something about him that's just got my hackles up. That's all."

He nodded. The DCI's instincts were sound; they'd helped crack enough cases. And the DCI had recruited the DI. He was prepared to give her a chance.

Besides, they didn't have anything else to do until Sophie got back.

If she did get back.

"Come on." The DI started moving across the driveway, her footsteps slow. The bloody gravel seemed to amplify every movement.

"We need to take it easy," he said.

"I know."

They moved across the front of the house towards the eastern side. From the plans of the place, he knew there would be a set of double doors from the kitchen, a patio looking out over the view towards Charmouth and the Isle of Portland in the distance. He looked up at the windows. No movement inside.

They rounded the side of the house. A red Toyota was tucked in by the building.

"Whose is that?" he asked. It was small and old; an 02 reg, not like the shiny new 74 reg out front.

She shrugged. "It's twelve years old."

People often bought their kids cheap cars, but Mhairi was miles away and hadn't been home in years. That didn't look like the kind of car her new husband would drive. And he'd seen the car before but couldn't remember where.

"I've seen it," he said.

The guv turned to him. "Here?"

He shook his head. "I haven't been here before. In Lyme. Maybe. I'm not sure."

She put out a hand to touch the bonnet. "It's warm."

Maybe it belonged to the man inside.

They continued moving, faster now that the gravel had been replaced by paving. The windows were just ahead.

The DI put up a hand, and Mike stopped moving.

She turned to him. "If it's a local, you've got a better chance of recognising him than I have."

He nodded and slipped past her. Slowly, he craned his neck to see around the doorframe of the closest patio door.

He had a clear view into the kitchen. A man sat at the vast granite-topped island, mobile phone in hand.

Mike's breath caught. He remembered.

He pulled back, his mind racing.

"It's..."

Jill had a hand on his shoulder. "Who?"

He frowned. What was the man's name?

"My... my mother-in-law's neighbour." He racked his brain. "Howard."

"Annie's neighbour? You're sure?"

Mike nodded. He didn't want to risk being seen again. And he was sure.

"It's him," he said.

But what was Annie's neighbour doing sitting in Sophie West's kitchen when Sophie herself was nowhere to be seen?

CHAPTER TWENTY-SIX

LESLEY LEANED back in her chair, phone pressed to her ear. The familiar voice of DS Dennis Frampton on the other end brought a mix of comfort and concern.

"How's the leg holding up?" she asked.

Dennis grunted. "Better, but still giving me grief. Retirement's not all it's cracked up to be."

Lesley smiled, despite herself. "You're missed around here, you know."

"Speaking of which," Dennis said, his tone shifting, "I heard a rumour Johnny's planning to come back. That true?"

Lesley sighed, rubbing her temple. "He's put in an application."

A pause on the line. "You think that's wise? After everything?"

"I'm not sure," Lesley admitted. "He left under difficult circumstances."

"That's putting it mildly," Dennis replied. "The lad was a mess."

Lesley frowned, recalling DC Johnny Chiles's final days

in Dorset. Dennis had found him at the home of organised crime boss Arthur Kelvin, sharing information in the hope that it would stop the Kelvins hurting his drug-addict brother.

Kelvin was dead now, but that wasn't the point.

"People can change, Dennis." And Johnny wasn't a villain; just stupid, sometimes.

"Maybe. But can the team trust him again? What will you tell them about him being in the Met for so long?"

Lesley glanced at the stack of emails in her inbox, Johnny's application at the top. "I haven't decided yet. It's not an easy call."

"Never is with these things," Dennis said. "Just be careful, boss. For everyone's sake."

She smiled. "I'm not your boss anymore, Dennis."

"Old habits die hard."

Especially with a dinosaur like Dennis. "Still. Give my best to Pam, won't you?"

"I will."

She hung up, shaking her head. She'd never made small talk with Dennis when he'd been her second-in-command. But now she was further removed from him, she felt she could open up more with the man. She might even describe him as a friend.

She barked out a laugh. Who'd have thought it?

Her thoughts were interrupted as Katie burst into the office, waving her phone ahead of her.

"Boss, I've got something," she said, breathless.

Lesley clicked onto another screen. "What is it?"

Katie slammed her phone onto Lesley's desk. "The planning applications. Roger Gallagher faked signatures on some of the planning committee records."

Lesley's eyes widened. "You're certain?"

"Yes. And there's more. Some applications were rejected after being approved in meetings. Sometimes it was the other way round. When Stanley cross-checked it against the bank account, there's a correlation with money going in. It all comes from another bank account in his name, in Jersey."

"Jersey?"

Katie nodded.

Lesley's phone rang. She answered, putting it on speaker. "Jill?"

"We're at Sophie West's," Jill said.

Lesley glanced at Katie. "Can she hear you?"

"That's the thing. She's not here, but her car's in the drive. But there's a man here."

Lesley exchanged glances with Katie. *A man?*

"Katie and Stanley have been digging into records," she said. "It seems Roger was taking bribes in return for either approving or rejecting planning applications, sometimes forging the signatures of other committee members."

"Wow. What else are we going to uncover about this bloke?"

Lesley leaned into the phone. "This man. Have you spoken to him?"

"No. We knocked on the door and he didn't respond. Mike thinks – Mike says – he recognises him."

"Who is he?" breathed Katie.

"Howard something. A neighbour of Annie's."

Lesley frowned. How deeply involved in all this was Annie Abbott? But Katie was scrolling through her phone.

"Guv," the DC said. "Is he Howard Murchison, Anning Road?"

There was muttering on the other end of the line. "Yes, that's him," said Jill.

Katie stared into Lesley's eyes. "His application was rejected. He wanted to build an extension."

"An extension?" *Surely you didn't commit murder over an extension?*

Katie nodded. "For his wife. They needed to make the house accessible after she had a stroke."

Lesley nodded. *So no ordinary extension then.*

"Jill," she said. "Do not enter the house. Get uniformed backup. And keep me informed."

CHAPTER TWENTY-SEVEN

JILL STOOD OUTSIDE THE HOUSE, her heart racing. The quiet of the calm wintry sea beyond the clifftops was in direct contrast to the churning in her stomach. She'd called for uniformed backup and was expecting PC Anderson and PC Sharman from Lyme Regis. She hoped that was enough.

Sharman and Anderson arrived in their patrol car and parked it in a cutting along the road. Mike went to the car and shook both officers' hands. Jill hung back. She was in charge here; no need to get too friendly.

"Ma'am," said PC Sharman. "What's the situation?"

Jill pointed back towards the West house. She had a thought.

"Mike, go and watch the house while I brief our colleagues here. I don't want him wandering off."

"Guv."

Mike hurried along the road. She resisted calling out an instruction to stay out of sight. He knew what he was doing.

She turned to PC Sharman. "We've got a potential

suspect in the Roger Gallagher case. He's inside Sophie West's house, that's the victim's widow."

"We know who she is, ma'am," said the PC. Her tone was curt, matter of fact. *Good.* Jill didn't need chumminess right now.

"Right. It's a Howard Murchison. He—"

"Howard?" said Anderson. Tina's brother-in-law, she reminded herself. "You're sure?"

"I'm sure. He's in the house, seemingly alone. It seems he may have had reason to want to harm the victim. Sophie's car is there, too, but there's no sign of her. I'm concerned he may have hurt her."

Sharman frowned then pushed her shoulders back. "You want us to get inside. Is there a warrant?"

"No, but we have reason to suspect someone inside that building is in danger."

"Of course. Come on, Dougie. You cover the back; I'll take the front."

He shook his head. "I know him. I'll knock on the door."

His colleague shrugged. "Fine." She glanced at Jill as she passed. "We'll try the gentle way first, then use force if we have to."

"Agreed." Jill followed them and stood at the end of the driveway, watching as PC Anderson knocked on the door.

He stood back and waited. Nothing.

PC Sharman reappeared from the side of the building. She approached Anderson and they muttered together. He nodded and the two of them threw themselves at the door, heaving all their weight into it.

It trembled but didn't open.

"Mike," Jill said, "you go round the side. I don't want escaping via the patio."

"The only route out that way is down the cliff."

"Just cover it, anyway."

"Of course, guv." He hurried away towards the house.

She could hear the voices of the two PCs at the front door. Sharman was instructing Anderson.

"On my count. Three, two, one."

They burst through the door. Sharman ran inside, heading straight for the kitchen where Jill and Mike had seen the man. Anderson hung back in the hallway, opening doors and calling out.

"Sophie! Sophie, it's the police. Are you here?"

Sharman's voice came from the kitchen. "DI Scott, you're OK to come in."

Jill pushed past PC Anderson and headed into the kitchen. Sharman stood by the island, gripping the man's arm.

"Howard Murchison?" Jill said.

Sharman nodded. "This is Howard."

He looked between the two of them, silent.

A shout came from the hallway. "Ma'am! I think she's upstairs."

Jill gave Sharman a look; keep an eye on him. She headed back into the hallway, where Anderson was halfway up the stairs.

"I heard a woman's voice, ma'am."

"Police!" she called up. "Sophie, you're safe now. You can come out."

What if they had it all wrong, and Sophie wasn't in danger? What if she'd been involved in killing her husband?

"She may be dangerous," she told Anderson.

"What?"

"We can't be sure if she's a victim, a witness, or a suspect."

Recognition flashed across his face as he pulled out a can of mace. "Right."

"But don't do anything rash," she said. This was probably the most excitement he'd got all year.

The house was eerily quiet. They took the stairs slowly, Anderson in front. One by one, he pushed the bedroom doors open.

She raised a hand at a sound; a woman's muffled voice. "In there."

Another door. Anderson tried the handle. Locked.

"Ms West?" he called. "Are you in there?"

"Yes! Help me, please!"

Anderson looked back at Jill, eyes wide. She narrowed her eyes; this could be a bluff.

"What d'you want me to do, ma'am?" he whispered.

"Open it. Kick it down if you need to."

He nodded. "Stand back, then." He tried the handle one more time, leaned against the door, then took a step back and aimed a kick at the wood beneath the door handle.

The door flew open.

Nice, thought Jill. Where did a Lyme Regis copper learn a trick like that?

Sophie huddled in the corner, eyes wide. Her arms were wrapped around her knees and the floor beneath her was damp.

Jill's gaze darted around the scene. No weapon. A red mark on Sophie's forehead, her hands trembling. She was clearly terrified.

"It's alright, you're safe now," Jill said, approaching with an outstretched hand.

Sophie's words tumbled out. "I recognised his face. You recognise everyone around here. But I'd never spoken to him before. He's never been to the house. Mark was out. He must have waited, because he knocked a few minutes later. I let him in and he..." She placed her fingertips on her forehead. "I don't know. But next thing I knew I was locked in here."

"Let me take a look at that. PC Anderson, call for an ambulance."

Sophie shook her head. "I'm OK." She leaned forward and threw out an arm for balance.

"No, you're not." Jill looked up at Anderson. "The ambulance, please."

He pulled out his phone. She turned back to Sophie. "I need to go downstairs and deal with him now. I'll leave you with PC Anderson and the paramedics will be here soon. OK?"

A nod.

Jill swallowed and pushed herself to her feet. She was stiff; she still hadn't got back into the habit of exercising after Suzi's birth.

"Right," she said. "Stay here."

Downstairs, Murchison was handcuffed to the back of a chair. Sharman stood next to him, watching him. By the look of it, she hadn't asked him any questions: sensible woman.

Jill took a step towards him. *All this, over a bloody planning application.*

"Howard Murchison," she said, "I'm arresting you for assault and false imprisonment. You do not have to say anything, but it may harm your defence if you do not mention when questioned something which you later rely on in court. Anything you do say may be given in evidence."

An arrest for murder would come later, she had no doubt. But she needed to get this man where he couldn't do any more harm.

CHAPTER TWENTY-EIGHT

Lesley stood in her new living room, surrounded by cardboard boxes. The sound of waves drifted through the open window. She shivered, knowing she should close it, but the sea air was oddly comforting.

She rummaged through a box labelled *Christmas*, searching for decorations. Her phone buzzed.

"DCI Clarke," she answered.

"Congratulations on the arrest, Lesley," said Superintendent Carpenter. His voice crackled through the speaker. "I hear he's been arrested for the murder, too."

"Don't give me the credit. It was a team effort."

"This is your job now, Lesley. You achieve results through them."

She grimaced, still not sure how she felt about that. She heard a rumbling sound and turned to see a large van pulling up outside, IKEA logo emblazoned on its side.

The furniture Sharon had chosen. She had no idea what to expect. *This had better be good.*

"Thank you, sir. We'll get a proper chance to celebrate in

the New Year. CPS will be charging him later today. Now if you don't mind, I need to spend some time with my family."

"And your new home. Of course, congratulations on that, too." He hung up.

The doorbell rang. She opened it to find Dennis, and behind him, Johnny.

Lesley's chest tensed. "I didn't realise you were down from London."

Johnny grinned. "Staying at my dad's for Christmas. Might be looking for a place." He gave her a long look, which she refused to answer with any comment about his application. It was still sitting on her system, waiting.

She swallowed. Should she support his application to return?

Before she could ponder further, Tina and Mike arrived, with Louis in Mike's arms.

"Housewarming present," Tina announced, thrusting a gift bag at Lesley.

"Thanks." Lesley wasn't used to gift bags. Was this what life would be like now?

In the kitchen, Tina cornered Lesley. "I don't mean to interfere, boss. But is it wise to bring Johnny back?"

Lesley froze. "How much do you know?"

Tina blushed. "All of it, boss."

Lesley turned back to the coffee machine, working through what had happened in her mind. It had been almost two years. She'd thought only Dennis knew about the blackmail.

She plugged the machine in and rummaged in a box for coffee grounds. As she stood up, tin in hand, the kitchen door opened and Elsa and Sharon entered, arms full of bags. Sharon gave her mum a quick kiss on the cheek, dropped her bag on the floor, and hurried out, barking orders at the IKEA delivery crew. Tina followed her out and into the living room, where it seemed the rest of Lesley's old team had taken up residence.

Elsa slid up to Lesley, a wry smile on her face. "Quite the flatpack mountain we've got to tackle."

Lesley groaned. "Don't remind me."

"You've got leave over Christmas, haven't you?"

"Yes, but I wasn't planning on using it to build furniture."

Elsa chuckled. "No rest for the wicked, eh?"

Lesley's gaze drifted to the living room. Johnny sat perched on a packing box, regaling the others with some London story. He looked comfortable. Too comfortable.

She watched as he threw his head back in laughter, the others following. She should join in. But she couldn't.

Carpenter didn't know why Johnny had left Dorset. She and Dennis had kept it between them, although somehow it seemed Tina had found out. The man's brother was a drug addict, and Kelvin had used that to get leverage on Johnny, to convince him to share details of police operations.

Two years in the Met looked like it had done him good. So why did he want to come back?

And would Lesley let him?

She still wasn't sure.

CHAPTER TWENTY-NINE

TINA SCANNED THE CROWDED BEACH. It was New Year's Day, and the Lyme Lunge was about to begin, locals packed in shoulder to shoulder.

"You ever done this thing?" Mike asked, jiggling Louis in his arms.

"No chance," she told him, pulling her gloves up tighter. "Have you seen my mum?"

"DC Abbott!" Annie's tones cut through the voices behind them, making half a dozen people turn.

Tina cringed, hating herself for feeling like she was fifteen again. The baby lurched in her stomach, and she put a calming hand on it.

"Shush, little one."

She turned and threw on a smile for her mum, who had four women with her. One of them was Rosamund, looking significantly less perturbed than she had last time Tina had seen her.

"Here we go," muttered Mike.

Annie pushed her way through the crowd, occasionally

stopping to exchange a joke with someone or to show off her floral swimming cap. Eventually, she reached them and grabbed Louis, holding him up proudly. One of the women with her, tall with messy dark hair, cooed at him. Behind her stood another woman in a boiler suit, hovering awkwardly.

"Let me introduce you all," Annie said. "Rosamund, you already know. This is Figgy and Helen from the swimming club. And Helen's partner, Finn." She frowned at the woman in the boiler suit. "*Not* dressed for the water."

Figgy, a large Black woman with an infectious grin, gave her a little wave. "Nice to meet you, Tina. We've heard a lot about you."

Helen threw back her head to laugh about something Tina knew nothing of, then thrust out a hand. "Tina. Mike. And little Louis. He's gorgeous."

Tina shook the woman's hand. It felt incongruous, shaking the hand of someone wearing nothing but a swimming costume and dryrobe.

"Helen's got a new project on the go," Annie said, eyebrows raised. "Something about babies?"

Helen's eyes lit up. "Oh yes! I'm collecting data on infant swimming reflexes. Fascinating stuff." She looked down at Louis, in Annie's arms. Tina reflexively grabbed her son back from her mum.

"It's alright, T," Mike said. "She won't do any experiments on Louis."

"It's only data collection," Helen said, her voice so loud Tina reckoned the whole of Lyme could hear her. "We drop them in cold water, always ready to help them out, of course, and see what they do. It's nature at its most raw and elemental." Her eyes were shining. "He'll love it."

Tina gave her mum a look. She put a hand on Mike's arm.

"Come on," Annie said. She threw off her poncho and thrust it at Tina, who barely managed to catch the thing. "Let's do this thing."

Annie was wearing a pink all-in-one swimming outfit that covered her entire body apart from her head and feet, and Tina couldn't help but think of Mr Blobby.

"Good luck, Mum," she said, arranging the poncho over one shoulder and Louis on the other.

Annie winked at her. "Thanks, love. But I won't need it."

THE POOLE HARBOUR MURDERS

DCI Lesley Clarke is back!

The dust has settled after the arrest of DCI Mackie's killer and Lesley has been told to make a few changes. She's got two DIs to manage, including one she's clashed with in the past, and is overseeing the return of a colleague who left Dorset under a cloud.

Just as she's starting to get to grips with it all, a body is found in Poole Harbour. Is it Jackie Kendal, who went missing a year ago, or Rowena Sharp, who mysteriously vanished after leaving her baby alone in a Sandbanks hotel in 1973?

Establishing the body's identity, and therefore whose case this will be, will require Lesley's investigatory skills and, more challenging, all of her tact and diplomacy.

The Poole Harbour Murders heralds the return of the much-loved DCI Lesley Clarke and her Dorset team in the award-winning series that's sold over a million copies.

Buy from book retailers or via the Rachel McLean website.

ALSO BY RACHEL MCLEAN

The DI Zoe Finch Series – buy from book retailers or via the Rachel McLean website.

The McBride & Tanner Series – buy from book retailers or via the Rachel McLean website.

The Cumbria Crime Series by Rachel McLean and Joel Hames – buy from book retailers or via the Rachel McLean website.

The Barn

The Lake

...and more to come

The London Cosy Mystery Series by Rachel McLean and Millie Ravensworth – buy from book retailers or via the Rachel McLean website.

Death at Westminster

Death in the West End

Death at Tower Bridge

Death on the Thames

Death at St Paul's Cathedral

Death at Abbey Road

The Lyme Regis Women's Swimming Club series by Rachel McLean and Millie Ravensworth – buy from book retailers or via the Rachel McLean website.

The Lyme Regis Women's Swimming Club

...and more to come